Thiess]

NNT-`

Part 2

The invisible enemy

-

Episode 1:

Target of the MD - Group

Preliminary information:

*The book is the suite of the previously published book 'NNT-Visions - An unforgettable and instructive journey into the mysterious experiences of life.'

** The story takes place in the USF (United State of Freedom). The USF consists of many states that have joined together after the war. Unlike in the US, different languages are spoken in the USF. Including German, English, French, Chinese and African dialects. One can imagine the USF as a mixture of different countries from different continents. The whole history and background of the USF are revealed in the course of the books.

In the USF, there are also some rules/laws that we are not used to. For the current episode, the following rules are of interest:

1) In the USF, the first name is also mentioned together with the doctoral title, e.g., Doctor Petra.

2) In the USF, names of clinics are freely chosen, regardless of the city or other.

3) In the USF, doctors are not required to show pregnant women pictures of their ultrasound during or after their examinations. Even on request, this can be refused. One of the many reasons for this is the ban on aborting children with disabilities.

4) In the USF, hospitals have a much larger problem of blood deficiency than with the availability of appropriate organs. The context of this situation will be explained later. But it has something to do with the previous war.

5) Villages without neighbors refer to places / islands included in the USF, but not formally owned by any USF state. They are often used by the Mark Dabrator group for private purposes.

6) In the USF, a conference in the context of education is organized once or twice a year. It is announced at very short notice by e-mail. Also here as with 4) the backgrounds are explained only later and have something to do with the terror at schools and Mark Dabrator.

7) If persons are reported missing, the USF has a minimum of twenty-four to thirty-six hours before the police intervene.

8) Employment relationships are always concluded by contract; even a private person, such as a babysitter, can only be hired with a written contract established in accordance with the USF law.

***These are the most important actors.

Berta: Biological mother of David and Beyonce.

Dr. Anne: Gynaecologist who helped Berta give birth. She is under suspicion.

Luc: Chief Inspector and Chief Investigator in the case of the abducted child.

Lea: Teacher and wife of Chief Inspector Luc.

Chris: Colleague of Chief Inspector Luc.

Dr. Petra: Colleague of Dr. Anne and wife of Chris.

Sebastian: IT expert and brother of Chris.

Elvira: Sebastian's partner.

Old lady: Strange appearance with a way of communication that takes getting used to.

Bill: Like Chris, he wears a tattoo of Mark Dabrator on his body and, like Berta, was a patient of the psychologist Dr. Lisa.

Mark Dabrator: A still unsolved mystery.

MD-Group = Mark Dabrator - Group

Exposé:

Luc is a very successful policeman. After the birth of his children, his marriage is doomed to failure. The shared dream with his wife of having a loving family threatens to burst after becoming the leading investigator in the Berta case. After some promising traces, he made himself and his family the target of a powerful enemy with extraordinary tricks. The circumstances force Luc to neglect the ongoing investigation just to save his family.

1 Luc looked at the yellow gerberas standing before him in a vase. He stretched his hand towards one of the delicate flower stems, then hesitated. These were Lea's favorite flowers. But shouldn't he rather buy classic red roses? A red rose wins the hearts of all women, doesn't it? Maybe that was true if we wanted to win back a heart?

"Can I help you?" the saleswoman asked.

Luc gave himself a discharge. He didn't need to win back Lea's heart. She only told him that yesterday. The last few weeks had been difficult, but now everything was fine.

"I would like to have the Gerbera," he said.

When he arrived at his home, he opened the front door, and a cloud of smoke rose towards him. Luc sniffed. The fire alarm went off, and Lea came out of the kitchen with the fire extinguisher. A thick cloud of smoke was escaping from the kitchen before she slammed the door. Luc deactivated the alarm and then coughed opening the living room windows. When he could breathe again, he approached her and took the extinguisher from her hand. "What happened?" he asked.

Lea burst into tears the next moment.

"I forgot the oil on the hot stove," she says softly.

Luc sighed with relief.

"As long as it's nothing worse," he said. "Look, I brought you flowers, darling." He took the Gerbera's bouquet, which had fallen to the ground in all the excitement and now seemed a little worn. Lea looked at the bouquet and burst into tears.

Then she turned around and ran to the room crying.

"Did I say something wrong?" asked Luc in silence.

He carefully pushed the door, which was ajar. He shuddered. The room was a mess. The bedding was crumpled on the floor, next to a framed wedding photo with broken glass. There were empty boxes of chocolate everywhere. Luc took a deep breath and approached the bed carefully where Lea was lying and crying. "What's the matter, darling?"

"Leave me alone," Lea shouted. She ran out of the room and slammed the door behind her. Luc heard Lea crying quietly outside the bedroom door. He approached the door. "Please talk to me, darling. You can trust me. No matter what happened, I'll always be by your side."

"I thought you loved me!"

"Of course!" Luc opened the door slowly. Lea had collapsed to the ground. He walked cautiously into the hallway and sat down in front of her. Lea looked down. "I loved you idolically! I trusted you blindly. And you?" She inhaled and exhaled deeply, then continued: "Why did you do that? How could you betray our great love? After all we've been through together over the years?"

Luc leaned forward and took Lea's hand in his.

"You know that you and our children are the most precious thing in my life. And it will always be that way."

Lea held still for a moment, then she pulled her hand back.

"Stop playing nice all the time! You're just such an idiot!"

"Please, Lea. Won't you finally tell me what happened?"

Lea turned her eyes away. Then she said in a quiet voice: "I have proof that you cheated."

Luc held his breath, then he laughed. He had already feared... but no, it was nothing serious — only one of Lea's fantasies.

Lea jumped up.

"How dare you laugh about it! If David, David, whom we have wished for so long, is not from me, but from... from Berta!"

"You're crazy!"

"No. The results of the maternity test are on the blue shelf in the bedroom. Convince yourself!"

Luc remembered his last conversation with Berta in which she had told him about Lea's intention to repeat the maternity test. Only at that moment did he realize that Berta had been right. It had been shocking enough for Luc to learn from a third that his wife had ordered a repeat of the maternity test behind his back. But much more shocking was the message behind Lea's testimony.

"Is Berta the mother of David?"

"Don't act so surprised," Lea shouted and contemptuously distorted the corners of her mouth. "That's of no use now."

Luc frowned. Could Chris be right? It all started when he took over Berta's case. When the suspicion arose, that Mark Dabrator had something to do with the abduction of Berta's children, Chris had warned him. Mark Dabrator, he had said, was dangerous. Anyone who opposed him was killed under mysterious circumstances shortly after. That, or he lost his fortune or was otherwise plunged into misery. At that time Luc had laughed. After all, he hadn't become a detective to avoid criminals, and Mark Dabrator was the most wanted criminal in the whole Republic. Slowly, however, he was overcome by the unpleasant suspicion that Chris had been right. Every time he made some progress with the investigation, something happened. First, his wife had received a strange letter, then pictures on her wedding day. How did he do that? Luc pressed a hand against his forehead. "Honey ...," he said.

Lea looked up.

"Please let us talk in peace."

Lea twisted her eyes. Then she went into the bedroom and came back with the results of the maternity test. She stretched them towards her husband.

"Here you go. Read it through and then tell me how you would feel if you were me?"

Luc accepted them hesitantly.

"How do you even know if the lab result is correct?"

"The test was checked and confirmed three times by different labs, so there's absolutely no doubt."

"Honestly, I can't explain how that happened."

"Save yourself the excuse. I want to live separate from you from now on. I need space."

Luc's heart swung between his belly and his brain. "What do you mean?"

"You already understood me correctly!"

Luc was silent. Then he said: "Don't you love me anymore?"

"What does that matter anymore? Even if I still love you, I don't have to put up with everything."

Lea took a deep breath. "I think it was all because of the doctor's findings."

"What are you talking about?"

"The report describing in detail why I had so little chance of ever getting pregnant." Luc shook his head in disbelief.

"You don't seriously want to accuse me of not having stood by you. I took a vacation to be with you. I helped you wherever I could."

"That's not what it's about!"

"What is it then?"

"Over the years you have told me again and again how important it is for you to have children. A being that carries your genes when you leave the earth."

"Yes and?"

"Quite simple: I believe that you cheated with the intention of conceiving a baby."

" Are you crazy?"

They stared at each other. Luc's heart was racing. "I don't want to listen to that any longer," he said. "I didn't cheat with Berta. That is all I have to say about it."

He left Lea and went into the living room. For a while, he just stood there without really seeing anything. Finally, he blinked. He took a bottle of whiskey from the drinks cabinet and drank a few sips straight from the bottle.

2. Lea sat bent over in the kitchen, her hands closed around a hot cup of chocolate. "I never thought love could be so poisonous to the soul," Lea thought. Maybe he just wasn't worth her love? She took a look out the window. It was already dark outside. The only thing she could see was the street lamp throwing her light on a small cutout of the sidewalk. She drank from the cup and put it on the table with trembling hands. How she hated Berta at that moment. What did she have that she didn't have herself? She was also pretty and dressed fashionably. And in bed, she was also a bomb or not anymore? With the back of her hand, she rubbed her burning eyes and then embraced her knees. What if Luc had told the truth? Maybe the tests were manipulated after all. Luc was still the same after all. Although they had been together for so long, he still looked at her the same way. Actually, he was always there for her. Would she not have noticed if he had cheated on her with another woman? He was a lousy liar anyway! She let her head sink into her hands. Had she overreacted? Did she have to blame herself? No, every woman in this situation would act the same as she did. That all had nothing to do with love and even less with marriage and the promise to be together in good times and in bad. She played on her wedding ring. She would love to take it off her finger and throw it away! He had broken a lot by breaking his wedding promise. She would never forgive him. Could she even imagine a future with him? Mockingly she pulled up one of her eyebrows. The right question was more likely, could she imagine a future without him? She took a look in the kitchen mirror at the spot above her breast, just below the collarbone where his name was tattooed.

"Dear God. Please help me," she said quietly. A movement in the mirror made her turn around. Luc stood in the entrance area. She was breathless. "How long have you been standing there? I thought you were asleep.

"Long enough to have listened to a large part of your monologue."

"Did you hear what I said?

"I did. Lea, I don't want to argue again. You have your opinion, which I respect. Sooner or later the truth will come out."

Lea made no sound, but tears flowed down her cheeks. Luc approached her and looked into her eyes. "Our love has survived earthquakes and thunderstorms of all kinds in the past," he said. "And now it should be different? Our love is a winner and does not let itself be struck down by hard blows of any kind! Perhaps I am the only one who now believes in another victory."

She replied his gaze in silence. Her lower lip trembled. "It hurts so much," she said in a breaking voice. "You promised me an eternal summer back then! And now?" When Luc reached out for her, she walked past him into the bedroom and locked the door behind her.

3.Chris wondered. For the first time since he knew him, Luc had appeared late at the police headquarters and disappeared without a greeting in his office. Well, everybody could be late at times, Chris thought and checked his e-mails. But when Luc still hadn't shown up half an hour later, and no noise came out of his office, Chris started to worry. He got up and made Luc a coffee, as a small compensation in case he does break into an important meeting, and then ran to his office. He knocked. No response. "Luc, it's me, Chris," he shouted. "Can I come in?" Silence. Chris carefully opened the door, a professional smile on his lips, which slipped a moment later. His colleague's office was already darkened early in the morning, and it smelled as if it hadn't even been ventilated. Chris turned on the lights and placed the coffee cup on the desk. "I can't believe it!" He watched his colleague for a while and shook his head in disbelief! "Luc, Luc ..." His colleague slept deeply and soundly. What was wrong with him? Chris leaned down over Luc and nudged him slightly. "Luc, wake up."

"What is it?" Luc said half asleep.

"What's going on? Don't you feel well?"

Luc stretched out. "All's well, thanks for asking," he muttered after yawning for a long time. Chris gave him a sharp look. "Really? Then what are the pills next to you for?"

"That's paracetamol and some tranquilizers. One can always need them." Chris raised an eyebrow. "If you don't want to talk about it, just say so!"

Luc sighed.

"It's about Lea," he said. "I think Mark Dabrator has his fingers in the pie."

Chris' heart cramped together. "Again?"

"I think so. I can't otherwise explain who is sending such destructive letters to my wife."

"Wait a minute. Has Lea received another anonymous letter?"

"Yes. Slowly I'm starting to believe that you were right. Maybe I should have left the investigation to another colleague."

"What did the letter say?" Luc pulled his smartphone out of his pocket. He scrolled up a picture and then held it out to Chris. "Here you go!"

Chris looked at the picture with his mouth open. "How did Berta react to it?"

"How should I know?"

"She is the babysitter of your children. You can't hide something like that from her."

"For your information, Lea has fired Berta and is now looking for a new babysitter."

"I almost thought so."

"She also told her she couldn't see the kids until everything was cleared up."

"Too bad. But understandable."

"Of course, I think that's a pity. But I couldn't afford to cause any more trouble in this situation by somehow trying to protect Berta." "Too bad, of course. "

Chris was silent.

"Well. Maybe it's better that way," Luc said. Chris frowned. "I'm not quite sure of your opinion on that."

"Why not?"

"If the sender of the anonymous letters is a member of the MD group, then I can well imagine that he has several goals."

"For example?"

"It may be that the sender wants to destroy your family. Or he's trying to cause a fight between your wife and Berta."

"The first possibility seems plausible to me. According to the motto: If you hunt us, we will destroy you. But I don't know what Dabrator wants to achieve with a dispute between Lea and Berta."

"Think about it. Geo was kidnapped because the Mark Dabrator clan assumed that he was Berta's biological child. If Dabrator overheard that Beyonce and David are actually their biological children, then he might be planning a new kidnapping." Luc bit his lip and scratched his stubble beard. "Lea also doesn't want me to meet Berta outside the police headquarters," he continued after a silence.

"That's not so bad. Berta has finally bought herself a mobile phone. She stopped by yesterday and left her phone number. You'll find it in the documents on her case."

Chris took a look at the clock. "I have to go back to my office. I still have some important e-mails to answer."

"Chris," Luc said, "Can I ask you a personal question?"

"What's it about?" Chris looked at Luc, but he avoided his gaze.

"Since the last conversation with my wife, I've been worried about this one night we were exceptionally at the beach club."

"I thought about that while I was looking at the pictures on your smartphone."

"I was so drunk I couldn't remember who I was talking to that night."

"I know. I had tried in vain to stop you. You were just so mad at your wife that you didn't listen anymore. You were drunk as a dummy, and then you left for a hotel room with three women."

Luc lowered his gaze. "That was really stupid of me. But I thought then that Lea had cheated. That is, of course, no excuse. I was just so angry. You know how much I love Lea. I would never intentionally hurt her."

"There is no doubt about that!"

"Now that she had received the letter, I wanted to ask if you remember the women with whom I went to the hotel room?"

"Yes. I remember the three faces well." Luc flinched. "Three women? Hopefully, Berta wasn't one of them. Or was she?"

"Don't worry. She wasn't there."

"Thank you. I really appreciate that you took the time to help me," Luc said relieved.

"Always happy," Chris replied and went to his office.

4. Lea slammed the apartment door behind her, and, in her haste, she almost lost all the tests she was holding on the left side. She had worked all weekend to get the correction done on time, then this morning she had completely forgotten about it and was forced to go home in her off-peak hour. So, what! Of course, it was only because of the fight she had with Luc yesterday. Lea opened the car door, threw her bag in the back seat and took the tests with one hand. As she turned to open the front door of the car, her gaze fell on the facade next to the front door. Lea approached slowly; her eyes narrowed.

"The truth cannot be seen by inexperienced eyes," was written on the facade, "Learn to recognize the invisible truth and wait patiently for it."

"What does that mean?" Lea's stomach was making a flip-flop. She looked around nervously. Then she took another look at what was written. "But who wrote such a thing? And why is it with different colors?" she asked herself. Quotation marks were in red, writing in blue. And everything was underlined in purple. She pressed her lips together and frowned. "Could red be related to blood? Purple stands for wisdom in our USF and blue for trust." She remembered a conversation with the old lady in which she heard something similar. "Eyes and strong emotions are the main causes of our blindness," the old lady said. Lea shook her head. Did the person who sent her the anonymous letter also attach the chalk text? And if so, what was the purpose? Did she perhaps want to point out to her that Luc was innocent after all? Her instinct was to give Luc a chance, but her mind excluded her husband's innocence. She was a math and physics teacher. She believed in numbers and facts, and a clinically confirmed multiple tests could not lie. The sound of a car rang out and shortly afterwards Luc turned towards the entrance of the garage.

"Hello, darling," Luc said and then stepped out.

"What are you doing here at this hour?" asked Lea. "I thought you were working longer today."

"I forgot some documents at home."

"Oh, I see. Then you'll leave right away?"

"Yes, and you? Shouldn't you be teaching?"

"Actually, yes."

"But?"

Silently, Lea pointed to the wall. "What does that mean?" she asked.

"I have no idea," said Luc, "but I guess the colors are not chosen by chance. Red represents either blood or courage."

"Aha. And what message could be behind all this?"

"The message is quite clear."

"I mean, with different colors."

"Perhaps red simply represents the courage to question the evidence. Courage not to prejudge people. Courage to give time a chance to correct misperceptions."

"Did you write that? Or how come you get into defense mode so fast?"

"Hahahaha. Very funny."

Lea was silent. She looked at him with an uncertain look. "I don't want to keep you too long. Thanks anyway."

"No problem."

"I'm gonna go back," she finally said.

"All right," Luc replied.

5 Berta sat in her bed staring at the opposite wall. She couldn't remember the last time she got up. Yesterday, maybe? But as hard as she tried, the only thing that came into her head was Lea's unexpected dismissal. Her eyes filled with tears.

How could Lea do such a thing to her? She had spent enough time with her to know that she was not a snake. How could she accuse her of having an affair with her husband? Moreover, the fact that she thought she had worked as a babysitter for her, only to continue flirting with her husband unnoticed, was even worse. She had never said it, but Berta had been able to read it in her eyes. Oh, she wished Lea could read into her soul. The only reason she liked working for her as a babysitter was because of the children. She could still sniff the smell of her little Beyonce on her and see David's irresistible smile as she sang his favorite song. How could she be so selfish? She knew how much the children loved her. Was Lea's ego more important to her than the joy of her children? Or was there more to it? She had often mentioned that she had the impression that the children enjoyed my presence more than hers. Could it be that this was one reason why Lea wanted to get rid of her? She sang a song she had always sung to the children with a tear-choked voice. She wiped her wet cheek. Why was sadness her faithful companion? "Was it yours too, Mama?" she thought. She had always been denied the chance to do something with her mother. And now her children should suffer the same fate? How many more generations would suffer like this?

"Didn't you know who my father was either?" she thought. Please, Mom, answer me. Does our curriculum vitae look the same? Is my life just an extension of a horror movie you played in before? Her eyes were red and swollen. She tightened the necklace of the rosary around her neck. Then she took a look at the Bible next to her pillow. "I know that no one is perfect, and I don't know the Bible very well either. But I read it from time to time, Lord, somewhere you say, "Ask, and it will be given to you; seek, and you will find; knock, and it will be opened to you."

Why doesn't that apply to me? Are there first and second-class prayers? Please, Father, free me from this burden. I don't want much. A family! I'm not eager for prosperity or anything else, just a life without too much pain.

Soon it will be Christmas. People say it's a celebration of love. They plan, make appointments and buy gifts. Children write wish lists to Santa Claus. I am now over thirty years old, and I have never had this privilege. The most beautiful gift I wish for is the feeling of being loved. Who better to convey this feeling than a loving and caring mother? Should my twins now suffer the same fate as me, and party without their mother? Is that right, dear father? Do my children and I pay for the sins of our ancestors?" Berta leaned her hand against her forehead. She had a slight headache. Then she searched her hair. She got up, ventilated her apartment and swallowed a paracetamol tablet. Then she went back to bed, leaned her Bible against her chest and whispered the twins' favorite song again until she fell asleep.

6 It took almost ninety minutes for Berta to be woken up by a nightmare. Her heart was about to jump out of her chest. She remembered part of her nightmare. Dr. Petra gave her children to someone and got something back in return. "What was that? She exchanges my children for a piece of paper. Was that a cheque?" She thought. "Next to Dr. Petra, there were 3 men. One of the men resisted handing over the child. Then he got into a taxi and drove away with one of the twins. While Dr. Petra screamed 'Bill stop, stop!' one of the other two men pulled out a gun and shot the taxi several times without success," Berta recalled. "What a stupid nightmare! Dr. Petra is a very kind gynecologist. She would never hurt a child," she persuaded herself. She heard her mobile phone ringing and took a look at it. "An anonymous call?" She paused for a moment and answered it. "Hello..."

"Berta," replied the caller.

"Yes? Who am I speaking to, please?"

"Post office. Your package has just been delivered. Thank you very much for your trust and goodbye."

"Wait a minute! I didn't order anything." All she could hear was a beeping sound. The caller just hung up. She shook her head in disbelief and took her mailbox key in her hand. She ran outside and emptied the full mailbox. One letter drew her special attention. The envelope was heavy and unmarked. She became curious. She put the other mail on the table in the living room and opened the heavy envelope first. She flinched. "That can't be true!" The first thing she saw were pictures. She wiped her eyes. "Pictures of Luc and me in a hotel? No, no. That can only be a bad joke." Her limbs froze. "Or maybe I have a twin sister?" Her palms became damp. She put the envelope and its contents on the table. She went into the kitchen and made herself a rosemary tea. She refined the tea with honey and lemon juice. Then she drank the still hot tea all at once and returned to the living room. She took the envelope back into her hands and read the message attached to the pictures. "It began generations ago! Your mother could have ended it. Unfortunately, she decided to end her life early instead. Now it's your turn. Do the right thing! Bring your twins to the given address at midnight. Don't press charges and persuade Luc to give up the cases around you. Be it Geo or something else...! Otherwise, the pictures and additional videos go into the public eye. The clock does not tick forever with us. Your mama already knew that." Icy fear tinged in her.

"The nightmare continues," she thought. "I can't go on any longer. Maybe I should revisit Dr. Lisa. She managed to calm my soul better than anyone else. Especially the exchange with others I found helpful at that time. I have the number of Bill. Maybe I should try it with him? I've helped him a lot in the past," she thought. "Meanwhile a friendly relationship developed between us. He could certainly distract me from all the stress," she continued. She pressed her mobile phone to her ear and waited for someone to answer.

"Hello!"

"Hello, Bill."

"Berta?"

"Yes. I hope I'm not disturbing you," she asked carefully.

"No, not at all. It's nice to hear from you. How are you?" Berta swallowed.

" I am not feeling well at all."

"What is going on? You don't sound good either. Did you cry?" Berta suppressed the already rising tears. "I just don't understand why my life is so complicated." For Bill, that wasn't the Berta who inspired him a few weeks ago with her "turning theory" and the good ability to play with thoughts. "What's the matter?"

"I just don't understand what happened in the past. How I got pregnant and who my parents are. Do they still live at all? Do I have siblings? Why did I live on the street?"

Bill was overwhelmed. He had only recently met Berta at Dr. Lisa's office, and now he was supposed to give her answers to questions about her past? A past he wasn't involved in.

"Berta, how did you come back on this subject now? Don't even think about it. Be positive, as you have been over the past few weeks. Do you still remember what you told me a few weeks ago?"

"Take life as it comes and make it the best it can be," Bill continued.

"Yes, I know. In fact, I had also left my past behind me."

"And why are you suddenly thinking about it? "

She remained silent. A few tears ran down her cheek. "Because my past does not leave me in peace. It's chasing me too much."

"What part of your past is chasing you?"

"I am the mother of twins."

"Yes and?"

"And the two children are from two different fathers."

"Seriously," replied Bill in amazement.

"I didn't even think it was that bad. What shocked me the most was the content of a letter I recently received by post. There were pictures in the letter. Pictures that show me with Luc in the hotel."

"It almost sounds like a bad April Fool's joke," Bill joked.

"I told you, no one believes me."

"But you and Luc, it's really hard to imagine. Do you think the pictures are true?"

"I don't know. Can you tell them apart?"

" Sometimes yes, but some images are so well forged that it is almost impossible to determine their authenticity without additional tools."

"I don't remember meeting Luc at the hotel."

"So, the images were manipulated."

"Do you know where I can get the photos checked?"

"Yes, near the police station of USF28-30."

"Where Chief Inspector Luc works?"

"No. That's not what I meant. Do you have a pen and paper? Then I can give you the address, and you write it down."

"Wait a minute."

While Berta was rummaging through her purse, Bill was thinking.

"I wonder what the connection is between these photos and your past."

"I've been asking myself the same question all along. Whether the pictures are true or not, I also wonder why they were sent to me now." Bill remained silent. He knew as little as Berta about what the sender was aiming for, but he had a bad feeling in the hollow of his stomach.

There is something else, Berta continued. "In the last few months, I've been employed as a babysitter by Luc and Lea. A few days ago, Lea asked me to accompany her to hospital B1 to get David's maternity test results."

"Chief Inspector Luc and Lea's son?"

"Yes, exactly. At least, that's what I thought."

"What does that mean now?"

"You must have heard about the baby swap at the Baby Born Clinic, right?"

"Yes, of course. The clinic where the babies were abducted and exchanged. The owner's name was Duc. It is now closed. You mean this clinic, don't you?"

"That's right. That's where my child was born. I say my child and not my twins, because at that time I had only one child, and I knew nothing about twins. All women who gave birth to their children in this clinic in the same month were forced, after a positive complaint from Chief Commissioner Luc and a request from the court, to register under the supervision of Dr. Albert at B1 Hospital. At the time of registration, a blood sample from the mother and baby was to be given. In addition, there were some tests that all mothers and babies had to do so that the responsible doctor could compare the data at any time and assign the babies to their biological parents. Strangely enough, I was David's mother and not Lea."

"The surprises really don't end, do they?" Bill said dryly.

"Yes, you could say it like that."

Bill formulated his next words very carefully. He was aware that he was moving on black ice. "It's strange. On the one hand, you learn that Lea's child is actually yours and on the other hand, you get pictures of you in a hotel with her husband. "

"I never had anything intimate with Luc!"

"Calm down, Berta. Even if others don't believe you, I believe you. I can't explain why, but I just believe you."

"Thank you. That means a lot to me."

Bill wrapped himself in silence. He wondered if he should tell Berta about the phone call, he just got this morning. It was just too many coincidences all at once.

"I know how you must feel," he finally said. "I was told this morning that I was the father of a girl I did not know. But I absolutely can't remember that either!"

"Hahaha. Great joke!"

"I mean it seriously. How could I joke about it in your current situation?"

"And how do you know that," Berta asked skeptically.

"I'm supposed to be the father of the little girl who was dying in the hospital. The newspaper said that she urgently needed a blood donation and her parents were not compatible. So, I decided to donate blood and save a life. But it was all anonymous. Nobody should know that I was the one who gave blood to the girl. The doctor assured me that he would not pass on my data."

"I didn't even know I was talking to a hero on the phone," teased Berta, but her voice had a warm tone. "And was the girl able to survive thanks to your help?"

"Yes. Dr. Albert contacted me and thanked me. He also told me that the girl was my biological child. So, now you know the story. And if you still don't believe me, we can go to Dr. Albert together and have it confirmed on the spot."

There was total silence at the other end of the line.

"Are you still there, Berta?" asked Bill.

"What was the doctor's name? Dr. Albert from hospital B1?"

"Yes exactly. Why do you ask so horrified?"

"I'm just curious, like most women," Berta replied, but her voice trembled. "When exactly did it happen?"

"A few weeks ago," Bill said.

Berta froze and remained silent.

"Are you still there?" Bill reassured himself.

She gasped audibly for air. "Can we meet?"

"Sure. Why not?"

"I mean right now!"

"I'd rather prefer tomorrow since I still have a few things to do at home."

"Apologies," she started hesitantly. "It is really urgent." Bill's eyes widened. "What is it all about?"

"I don't want to talk about it on the phone. But if you can't find time today, I'll wait until tomorrow." Bill rubbed his nose nervously. "Well, guess we can still meet today. When and where?"

"As fast as you can. I would send you the address by SMS. Okay?"

"All right."

"Thank you. See you later."

Bill put his cell phone on the table in front of him. He slipped restlessly back and forth in his armchair. He speculated about the background to this very spontaneous meeting with Berta.

"What could be so urgent? Is there a connection with my blood donation in the clinic? Or does she want to talk about my tattoo and Mark Dabrator again? He pulled his brows together. "Does she want to talk to me about a possible connection between Dr. Albert and the MD group? After all, that's the only subject she ever addressed when she wanted to talk to me urgently." He then prepared himself and went to Berta.

7 Bill arrived a little earlier at the agreed address. Berta had suggested a meeting in a quiet bar. He went in and ordered a fruit juice with apples, melon, oranges, and mango.

"Mama was right. This fruit mixture is really balm for the soul, " he said after a few swigs. Bill bridged the time waiting for Berta with his smartphone. Suddenly two strange women approached him. "Gentleman, may we join you?" Bill frowned.

"I'm sorry. I have an appointment."

"Come on. At least a glass of wine?" Bill scratched his beard and looked at the women inquiring. They were barely clothed. Half her bottom looked out of the much too short trousers, and her bra was transparent. The women smelled of alcohol and cigarettes. "Maybe another time," he finally said with a smile on his face.

"But we want to get to know you better. The last time was too short." Bill looked at the women confused.

"Have we seen each other before?"

"Of course. About a year ago," one woman replied while the other looked for a picture in her smartphone. Thoughtfully Bill closed his eyes. "You must be mistaking me for someone else."

"No wonder! When you're drunk, and probably on drugs, everything looks similar," he thought afterwards.

"Look at that," asked one of the women.

"You are the man on the right in the picture, aren't you," reassured the other woman. Bill couldn't believe his eyes. It began to rustle in his ears.

"Luc, Berta and I in one picture," he whispered thoughtfully.

"Luc and Berta. So that's the name of your two friends," one of the women inquired.

"Yes! Where and when was that?" he choked out.

"Hotel 'MD' a few feet from the beach club. We used to work closeby."

"As what, if I may ask?"

"At the Beachclub. Are we drinking together now?"

Bill saw Berta come in.

"I'm sorry. I'd like to give you two glasses of wine, but only if I can have your contact details?"

"Of course! Here's our business card."

"Thank you." Bill put the business card in his wallet and said goodbye to the women. Shortly afterwards, Berta took a seat next to him.

"Hello, Berta."

"Hello, Bill. Sorry for my delay. I hadn't expected so much traffic."

"No problem. What do you want to talk so urgently with me about that it can't wait until tomorrow? "

"About your blood donation." Bill followed her action and saw her get a newspaper article out of her handbag.

"Look at the picture."

"So what?"

"That's what you're talking about, isn't it?"

"Exactly. I gave blood to this girl."

"And recently you heard from Dr. Albert that she was your daughter. Right?"

"Yes. Why do you care so much?"

"Because she is my daughter!"

Bill's heart clenched. "Wait a minute, are you serious?"

"Yes. Beyonce is our daughter together."

Bill shook his head in disbelief. "Beyonce is Luc's daughter."

"No. Back when he wanted to donate his blood, it turned out he wasn't Beyonce's biological father."

Bill didn't know what to say. The shock was so great that he got up, settled his bill and left the snack bar without saying goodbye. Berta took her bag and followed him to his taxi.

"Wait a minute, Bill!"

"What then?" Bill scolded.

"I'm just as surprised and shocked as you are. I don't know if I suffer from a memory loss, but I don't remember ever meeting you before Dr. Lisa's session either."

"Neither can I. But it's true."

"How do you know that?"

"Shortly before you came, two women were with me. They showed me a picture of the three of us."

"The three of us?"

"Luc, you and me."

Berta took a short breath. "When and where was that?" she inquired further.

"According to the women about a year ago and at the hotel 'MD.'"

"If that's true, then the pictures I got are definitely real. They're also from the hotel "MD" next to the beach club."

"You mean the pictures of you and Luc at the hotel?"

"Yes. But why can none of us remember it?"

"Good question!"

"Is it possible to turn off certain memories?"

"I already heard something about it in my childhood. My father said that there was a dangerous group that would be particularly good at such things and would use them more often for selfish purposes."

"That sounds like Mark Dabrator."

"That's what I thought. But right now, I can't think so well. I have to go home and rest for a while."

"I understand that. Contact me later, when you have strength and desire again."

"Everything is clear and thank you for your understanding." He hugged Berta, got into his taxi and drove home.

Bill went home in his cab. Lost in thought, he steered his car safely forward in traffic. "I have a daughter. How can that be? I thought after the destruction of my family I didn't have any blood relatives. A loud horn ripped him from his thoughts. Frightened, he looked around. He noticed that the car behind him started honking again. He noticed that the traffic light was changing from green to red at that moment. "Shit," he said out loud. "What the hell. It's going to be green again." A smile briefly brightened his eyes. "The news comes as a surprise. But the thought itself is beautiful. Every man can only wish to have a child with a loving wife like Berta." He swallowed. "The only problem is that if the man behind the murder of my whole family finds out... He wanted to destroy all our blood relatives." The traffic light turned green again. Bill stepped on his gas pedal as hard as he could and drove off. His car squeaked. "I'm only alive because I'm safe with the protection of this secret group I've belonged to since my last attempted murder. Should I perhaps inform Berta about this now? How else could I justify the fact that I would let the girl be protected for a while?" He took a deep breath. "According to the original agreement, nobody should know that I belong to this group. What am I going to do?" Bill took a right turn a few meters from his apartment. "It may be that the enemy of my family has found out about it and wants to hurt my child. Luc is a policeman, but such people don't let themselves be impressed by it. I urgently need to talk to Luc and Berta. I have the feeling that something could happen to my daughter soon." He had arrived. He stopped his car and stayed seated. He did not move. He chewed on his lip. "I must first talk to the leader of my secret group. She knows Mark Dabrator and his partners very well. Maybe she has a good tip for me."

8 It was early in the morning. The birds chirped, and the first rays of sunshine shone in Berta's room. She breathed in and out deeply once more and then put her sleeping mat on her side. She took her water bottle and drank a big sip. She wasn't hungry, but for health reasons, she had to eat something. Berta suffered too much from the loss of appetite and weight loss in the last few days. If she didn't eat again soon, she could have collapsed at any time. She was aware of that. She pressed her hand against her forehead. "Well. I have to eat something," she thought. The doctor had recommended her nerve-boosting food. But she didn't feel like eating chocolate anymore. She wanted fruit, except bananas. She opened the fridge to see what she actually had left. She took out a paprika. This could help her reduce her fatigue. She took a vegetable knife and cut the peppers into small pieces. She kept losing her head in the process. Consequently, she injured herself with the knife. "Ouch," she screamed. She put a plaster on her wound and sat down on a chair. What kind of mother was she anyway? She worried about strange meals and worries about her health. But what about her children? Were they well? How would she know that Lea was good with them since it was clear that she was the mother of the twins? Should she instead go to Lea? On the other hand, she would certainly not let them in. But wasn't the love for her children worth a try?

"Yes, yes, yes," Berta convinced herself. She ate a few pieces of paprika and then left the kitchen. She had brushed her teeth and combed her hair quickly. Then she put on her shoes and spontaneously went to Lea. During the ride, she imagined different scenarios for a new meeting with Lea. "I'm sure Lea will be furious when she sees me. She will accuse me again that I only came to see her husband. Well, I don't care! If she wants, she can continue to insult me. If I can see that my children are well, then I will go back home very happy. But what should I do if she does not allow me to see the children? She felt desperation rising inside her. "Violence against Lea is out of the question. She is a hobby martial artist. Well, at least I could file a complaint."

"We have arrived at our destination," said the taxi driver. Her heart pounded up to her throat as she got out of the taxi and approached the front door.

9 She was outside Lea's front door. She put her hand on the bell, but then hesitated. "Come on, Berta. You can do it! The love for your children overcomes every obstacle," she convinced herself and finally pressed the bell.

"Yes?" Luc answered at the hands-free car kit.

"Hello, Luc. It's me, Berta."

Luc unlocked the door by pressing a button. He blinked violently. "Hello, Berta. What are you doing here? I thought you had been discharged by Lea."

Berta was silent. Her eyes filled with tears. "Yes. May I please see my children for a moment?" she finally said in a breaking voice.

"I am sorry. I can't afford that right now."

"What does that mean?"

"Actually, I'm only home because Lea asked me to this morning. She had to go to the doctor. Since we don't have another babysitter yet, I have to take care of the children until Lea comes back. If she catches you here, I really can't guarantee anything."

"Please just for a moment. I'll be gone in a minute."

He looked at the clock and went through his hair. "Fine. But please hurry.

"Thank you! You have a beautiful soul," burst out of her. She rushed into the living room with a broad grin, where the babies lay on their mat on the carpet. Luc observed at a short distance how happy the twins were to have the opportunity to play with her. She sang the children's favorite song. Luc approached them quietly. He was touched by the atmosphere Berta was able to create in such a short time. The broad smile on her face and the noises of the children, which they gave off with joy, brightened his wet eyes. He enjoyed the moment so much that he forgot the time. Then he heard someone open the door. He took a deep breath.

"Berta, my wife's back."

Before Berta could answer anything at all, Lea entered the apartment. There was silence. When Lea took off her shoes in the entrance area, she recognized Berta's shoes. "What are these shoes doing here?" she yelled and hurried into the living room. When she entered the living room, only the babbling of the children could be heard. Luc stopped. He went through his hair again and smiled at his wife, embarrassed. Berta stood up without comment and waved farewell to the children with a freezing smile. Lea was stunned. She felt like in a nightmare. She stopped at the entrance of the living room and watched the whole thing with a rapid heartbeat. "Great! As soon as I'm gone, it's enough to see her," Lea said. Her voice almost rolled over.

"Please don't start that again," Luc commented.

"You better remain very quiet for now!"

"What then? He is right, after all. You accuse us of something which is not true at all," Berta defended herself as well.

"Excuse me, Madam! The supposedly quiet Berta is already making big noise, isn't she? "

"How can I prove my innocence if I remain silent," Berta continued.

"Oh what. Am I the culprit then? Are the doctors of many years who confirmed that you have a child together suddenly stupid? Is it pure coincidence that our children are almost the same age," Lea replied. She cooked inside and clenched her fists several times and opened them again. She was afraid to scare the children or to hurt them unintentionally. Her eyes filled with tears. She looked briefly at Luc and disdained the corner of her mouth. Then she turned to Berta with flaming eyes. "You tell everyone how sad you've been for the last thirty years. Is it perhaps because you have never appreciated love? Or is love rightly afraid of you?"

"You don't have to insult me. I have not chosen my destiny. And why should love be afraid of me? I have never intentionally hurt anyone."

" You did. Do you know what my husband means to me? No, of course not!"

"I swear, I never had anything with your husband," Berta repeated loudly.

"He is there after all. Ask him, " she added.

"How many times should I tell you? Berta and I never had anything intimate with each other," Luc underlined Berta's statement.

Lea narrowed her eyes. "Why am I doing this to myself at all? This conversation is torture for my nerves. Berta, please leave my house immediately and never come back!"

"I would never come again if you tell me where I can see my children in the future."

"This is only possible after a court agreement. Besides, it's only possible when the clinic returns my biological children to me. If Geo is one of them, find him. Only then can the court proceedings begin."

"Yes, I have informed myself about that. I was by MixSKids."

"What the hell is that?"

"MixSkids is a court that takes care of underage children," Luc briefly explained to his wife.

"Exactly. And if you deny me of seeing my children, I will file a complaint there," Berta threatened.

"Should I be afraid because of that?"

"You should think about it! "

Lea swallowed. She opened the apartment door and asked Berta to leave the apartment again by hand movement. Then Lea took the children with her into the bedroom. Luc left the apartment and went to work.

10 After the dispute with Lea, Berta drove straight back home. She switched off the insults Lea had expressed to her. She focused on love for her children and what she should do for them. As Lea sounded, she would not engage in a peaceful solution. At least not without a court order. She chewed her fingernails. "Well, if she wants to clarify it by judicial means, then so be it! It will certainly be a hard fight," she thought. She leaned back and frowned slightly. Maybe support would be necessary. But who could help her? The fathers could also make their contribution. Luc could be very helpful as an experienced policeman, but his wife will certainly stop him. Or not at all? David is also his son. But Berta was more worried about Beyonce. After all, she was not allowed to live with her biological parent. Maybe she should talk to Bill about it? That would certainly make sense. But before that, she would have to learn more about him. What kind of person was he anyway? Could her daughter be safe in his hands? After all, he had the tattoo "Mark Dabrator" on his back. "What if he belongs to this group? Could it be that he is pretending to be friends with me in order to have easier access to my privacy and to kidnap my daughter later more easily?" Berta thought. She realized she needed to know more about Bill. The only question was who could help her. She certainly couldn't afford a private detective. She massaged her head. Then she took a pack of nuts out of her handbag and ate some. "How else can I learn more about Bill? Should I perhaps pretend love to him in order to get more important private information faster? Her cheeks got hot. She stared at the ceiling. No. That would be immoral. Recently Lea accused her of not appreciating love. If she did that with Bill now, God would agree with Lea. Suddenly she turned her lips into a thin smile. "Now I know! Dr. Petra could help me. She certainly knows more about Bill than I do. She already had this feeling during the last conversation with her: "I have to call her as soon as I'm home. Hopefully, she can tell me something important."

11 About a week later, Berta and Dr. Petra met outside the clinic after a telephone agreement in order not to be overheard. Berta arrived by bicycle. As she descended, she saw Dr. Petra already standing in a dark corner of a quiet side street. She looked around to make sure no one was watching her. Then she ran to Dr. Petra. When she arrived at her, she was out of breath. Dr. Petra said nothing and instead showed her that she should be quiet. They went to a restaurant next door together. Arriving there, Berta finally had her say. "Thank you for taking the time to meet."

"No problem. I was quite surprised by your call, but I can imagine what the problem is and why we are meeting."

Berta pulled up her eyebrow. On the phone, she had just told Dr. Petra that it was something urgent. She didn't dare directly address the actual reason for her meeting. At first, she only mentioned what Dr. Petra probably suspected. "It's about the twins."

"That's what I thought," she said dryly. For a moment both women were silent before Dr. Petra broke the silence. "I can't tell you much more either. You already know that the twins are from two different fathers. But I can't help you find the fathers. My medical secrecy doesn't allow that."

"That is no longer my problem," Berta said briefly. "I already know who the fathers are."

Dr. Petra looked up. "May I ask where you got this information?"

"I just accidentally learned it during a phone call."

"Oh, and of course you know who your children are?"

"Of course! David and Beyonce."

"So, Luc is the father," Dr. Petra asked with a frozen face. "Don't get me wrong: I'm asking this because my colleagues did a paternity test for David after the incident with Beyonce and at Luc's request. And it was positive." It went exactly as Berta had wished. Finally, she had a good opportunity to introduce the Bill name in the conversation.

"Yes, Luc is the father of David and Bill is the father of Beyonce."

"Bill, the taxi driver?" she asked tonelessly. A muscle in her face twitched.

"You know him?"

Dr. Petra lit a new cigarette with trembling fingers and took a deep breath.

"It doesn't matter whether I know him or not," she finally said.

"This isn't the first time you've behaved strangely when I'm talking about Bill."

"As I've told you before, I've had bad experiences in the past with someone called that."

"Hmm," Berta said.

"How do you even know the information is true? Have you already had the claim confirmed by a doctor?"

"It's none of your business," Berta replied angrily. "If you don't want to answer my questions, I see no reason to answer yours. Two can play this game."

"Wait a minute. You asked me to meet you. I came here to help you, not to talk about my private life."

"Exactly. And if you have any information about Bill that I don't have yet, it would be very helpful if you could share it with me."

Dr. Petra took a deep breath. "You've already said that! "

Berta angrily crossed her arms in front of her chest.

"Every time I talk about Bill, her body language changes. She seems paralyzed for a moment. Moreover, she asks me to speak more quietly, as she has just indicated with her gesture," Berta thought to herself. "Why do you make this gesture when I'm talking about Bill?"

"I've already replied to that. That's all I can say." Dr. Petra took one last draught of her cigarette, crushed it under her heel and turned to walk.

"What are you doing?" Berta asked in horror.

"What does it look like?" the gynecologist replied without even looking at her.

"We're not finished yet," said Berta, who walked next to her.

" We are. Originally, I thought you needed help. But now I know that you only want to snoop in my private life."

Berta blocked her way.

"Excuse me. If I pressed you with my question, it was not intentional. Maybe I overreacted. Please let us continue the conversation."

"All right," Dr. Petra finally said. " Let's do it quickly. So, do you have any medical evidence that Bill is really the father?"

"He's the unknown person who donated blood when Beyonce was in hospital B1."

"I understand. If you already know all this, then how can I help you?"

"I wanted to ask how that could be. How can I get twins from two different...? "

"This question is also complicated for me to answer. I'm afraid you'll have to wait a little longer. We will soon find the right answer."

"You sound very sure! Do you know more?"

Dr. Petra hesitated. "I have a clue," she said, "but I ask for your understanding that I can't tell you anything yet."

She had drawn her eyebrows into two steep lines. She seemed worried.

"Did you find anything else in the clinic I don't know?"

"Yes. I have read some of Dr. Anne's papers. I think she meant well."

"Oh yeah? That's what I thought at first. But now I really don't remember. She hasn't contacted me, and the mobile phone number she gave me isn't valid."

"She called me."

"And why do you think she meant well?"

"I can't say much, but she mentioned that your babies were expected and had to be delivered after birth."

"Delivered? To whom then?" Berta asked frightened.

Dr. Petra laughed. "You can probably best answer the question yourself!"

Berta noticed that Dr. Petra's handbag was slightly open. Right now, the doctor looked inside and then looked at Berta intensively as if she were comparing her to someone. "Are you listening to me at all?" she asked, "What are you doing?"

Without making a comment, Dr. Petra closed her handbag, pulled her mobile phone out of her jacket and called Berta over her shoulder while she was already standing up. "Give me a few minutes, I need to make a quick phone call. I'll be right back."

12. It took exactly seven minutes for Dr. Petra to return. Berta knew because she had stopped the time.

"Who brought you food when you lived on the street and were pregnant," Dr. Petra asked abruptly as she stood in front of her again.

Berta was angry. It was incredible how the woman dealt with her! First this strange body language and the evasive answers and now this pushiness!

"No idea. What makes you think so?" Berta groaned.

"Be honest! Who gave you a room after the third month in which you lived without having to pay rent? And without having to buy food or anything else? In a village where there are almost no neighbors and no shops? Why did you claim to have spent your pregnancy on the street? You can lie, but you can't lie to yourself! right?"

Berta's heart beat faster. "How do you know all this?"

"That's not important at the moment. Much more important is that the one who helped you is probably pursuing a goal."

"Did Dr. Anne know the same?"

"I don't know exactly." Berta's hands were sweating. Instead of taking a handkerchief out of her trouser pocket and wiping off the cold sweat, she secretly wiped her hands off her trousers. She suddenly felt paralyzed.

"Are you all right," Dr. Petra broke the silence.

"Yes, I am fine. "

Dr. Petra's cell phone rang. She took it out of her jacket pocket, looked briefly at the display and pressed a button. The cell phone fell silent, and she put it back in her jacket pocket. "Unfortunately, I have to go," she said. Berta tried to pull herself together. "Thank you for your time," she said.

"Bye."

"Goodbye."

13 Like Berta, Sebastian was also very concerned about his daughter Lea. He pressed the bell at Dinkelweg 51. His right hand was already aching from the weight of the briefcase; however, he did not put it down, but held the handle tightly. Chris opened it. "Sebastian," he shouted in a good mood. "It's good that you're here!"

"Thank you, brother," he replied with a smile and followed Chris into the apartment.

Only in the kitchen did he put the luggage down and stretched out his half-brother's hand. "How are you?"

Chris replied with a crooked smile and offered Sebastian a seat at the dining table.

"What can I offer you? Water, tea or coffee?"

"A glass of cool water. It'll do me good after the heat outside."

Chris handed him the glass and sat down opposite him. He looked at him anxiously. "You sound different than usual."

Sebastian did not answer. They both knew that the situation he was in was anything but not ordinary.

"Wow! Your suitcase is almost as big as my table," Chris joked.

"Rightly so. It contains a lot."

"May I learn more about the content?"

"Don't worry, it's not a bomb."

Chris smiled and replied. "It's nice that you haven't lost your sense of humor despite the emotional strain."

"Do you think so?"

"Yes."

"Fun aside. The suitcase contains details of the security measures I suggested to you during the last interview." "Yes." He opened the suitcase and pushed it to Chris. Chris looked at some documents.

"Oh so. What's so special about that again?"

"It's a product I'm developing with a drone factory. At the moment the cameras can take very good pictures up to a distance of five hundred meters. We are also building so-called "DrohnenH" drones. "

"What does that mean?"

"These are stops for drones. You can park moving drones there if the battery runs low. It is also possible to carry and park several cameras. One advantage is that if a camera breaks down due to vandalism, you can change it more quickly. Another advantage is the mobile function. For example, if we recognize my daughter on a video, we can follow her. The drones are very small and at a certain distance silent and absolutely inconspicuous."

"I am impressed brother. I know that drones exist, but you have now made it clear to me how we can use them skillfully for our investigations."

"I'm pleased."

"I still have to talk to Luc and my boss Geral about this. Only if Geral agrees, we can use them", Chris commented.

Sebastian gave his brother a questioning look.

"How's the investigation going? Are there any leads yet? A hair left behind by the kidnapper or a fingerprint. Something, you know ..."

Chris leaned on the kitchen table. "Sebastian, now listen to me," he said.

"You know I can't tell you anything. Believe me, I know what you have to go through, but should it come out that I have betrayed any of our investigations, I'll lose my job." He must have looked very disappointed because Chris continued without pausing: "But I can assure you that we are doing our best to close the case successfully. You know you're not the only one in this situation."

"I never doubted that you would do your best," Sebastian said and ran through his hair with both hands.

"It's just the uncertainty that's driving me crazy."

"I know, brother. I promise you that I will do everything in my power to find your daughter again."

Sebastian's eyes were burning. He swallowed and blinked away the tears that threatened to rise. "I really appreciate that."

"You, what do you think of us going into the living room and turning on the TV," Chris said in an unnaturally cheerful voice into the silence. "Football should start now. You are a football fan, aren't you? We can order pizza later and still have beer in the fridge!"

"Thank you," Sebastian said, "but I think it's better if I go."

"Are you sure?" Chris said.

Sebastian rose. He couldn't bear Chris' worried look any longer.

"For sure. Thank you for the water."

14 Sebastian entered his apartment. Elvira sat in the living room chair and leafed through a magazine. For some reason he had the feeling that she had just been waiting for him.

"Hello honey," she said and stood up. "How was your day?"

Without looking at her, Sebastian walked past her. "I don't want to talk about it."

"You were with Chris again, weren't you?" Her voice trembled. "You let this thing drive you completely crazy. You don't care what happens to us!"

Sebastian stopped. He turned around and said, "This thing you are talking about is the kidnapping of my daughter!"

"Oh honey! I know how hard all this is for you. But it's time you accepted the inevitable. We received the letter seven weeks ago. Chris said that in all known cases the persons were not alive after four weeks. Your daughter is ..."

"My daughter's alive," screamed Sebastian. "I am sure that she is alive. I would have felt it if anything had happened to her!"

Elvira looked at him. Her lower lip trembled. "Believe me, I want to believe as much as you do that, she is alive. But maybe ..."

"There's no such thing as maybe," Sebastian shouted. He was aware that he was screaming, but at that moment he was indifferent.

"Stop your funny way of thinking! There is not even any evidence that the letters are really from Mark Dabrator! And secondly, if I may remind you, it is also extraordinary to receive a letter from Mark Dabrator when the child was sacrificed. When we received the letter, we were well rewarded and immediately after receiving the letter. This simply means that the person was already quite satisfied. It was different with Dr. Petra and my brother Chris. They also received a letter without receiving a single reward".

Elvira fell silent. Then she said: "I don't want you to get unnecessarily false hopes."

"One can always count on your support," Sebastian said sarcastically. "Slowly I have the feeling that you don't care about Lea at all!"

He walked past Elvira, fetched a bottle of whisky from the drinks cabinet and drank a few sips straight from the bottle.

Then he fetched the photo album from the drawer and stormed past the frozen Elvira from the living room. He stopped in front of the door of Lea's room. He hesitated. He hadn't entered her room since she disappeared. The idea of going in and finding only an empty room hurt him too much. Slowly he pushed the door handle down and opened the door. He needed a moment before he was collected enough to take a step into her room. His heart pounded painfully. Everything was the same as the day he last entered her room. The whole room smelled of her. He suddenly felt closer to her than he had in a long time. He put the photo album on her desk and sat down carefully on her bed. He took her teddy bear in his arms and pressed him tightly to himself. When she was a little girl, he had bought her a teddy bear while taking a walk in a shop. He remembered exactly how she stood in front of the shop window and desperately wanted this one teddy bear and the joy in her eyes when she had taken him in her arms. He took him and kissed him on the nose. "Don't worry! She'll be back soon," he comforted the teddy bear with tearful eyes. Then he lovingly laid him back in her bed and covered him up. His gaze wandered on to the wall next to her bed, which was decorated with many photos. His daughter had hung photos of them both with many hearts. Under a picture was written: "You are the best daddy in the world". He remembered the evening on her second birthday when she had asked about her deceased mother and he gave her his promise to always be there for her and to protect her. At that moment he realized that he had made her a promise he could not keep. He looked through the window into the dark sky and inwardly asked God for help. Then he lay down exhausted in her bed and fell asleep.

15 Bill made his way to the place where he had an appointment with the leader of his secret group. As required by the laws of the secret group, the appointment was met very punctually by both sides. In addition, members of the group were asked to refrain from greeting them and from making any inconclusive statements.

The motto was: "Summarize the most important things in the shortest time!"

Bill was already familiar with the protocol. He already knew where to sit. He also remembered that he should not speak before her.

"What is it about?" she started the conversation.

"About the protection of my daughter."

"Is she in danger?"

"From my gut feeling, yes."

"Where is she now?"

"With Chief Inspector Luc and his wife Lea."

"I'm sorry. But it's impossible for us to guarantee one hundred percent protection."

Bill wrestled his hands in excitement. "What am I supposed to do now?"

"Bring the girl here once."

He cast out a desperate blow of breath. "How is that supposed to work? I don't officially have custody yet. Besides, I don't know Luc or Lea privately in order to have access to my daughter at all."

"And her mother?"

"Berta. Maybe she could see the child. But she would never agree to bring her here."

The leader, whose real name Bill was also unknown, opened a drawer. She took out one of hundreds of chains and gave it to Bill.

"What am I supposed to do with it?"

"Try to hang the chain around your daughter's neck. Either way, personally or hand it over to someone who can do it for you."

"Can I use it to protect her from the group without bringing her here once?"

"Yes," she confirmed thoughtfully.

"How is that supposed to work? The chain doesn't have a GPS, does it?"

"No. At that age GPS might be dangerous for the child. GPS are also very common. So also, conspicuous. True protection takes place unnoticed. The chain consists of a special material mixture that we have developed over many years. It is only known to a few people so far."

"What is special about the material mixture?"

"Depending on the lighting conditions, the chain radiates a different color, which can only be recognized up to two hundred and fifty meters away with certain glasses. Our security personnel have been trained accordingly by our developers. They were given a table with instructions as to which glasses to use in which lighting conditions."

"So, the chain helps to locate the child up to a distance of two hundred and fifty meters? Even when clothes are over the chain?"

"Yes. Except for very wet clothes. But that would almost never happen to a child at that age."

"Thank you." The most important thing was clarified. Bill continued to follow the motto of the group.

He stood up and left the room without further comment.

16 Bill turned his cell phone back on after talking to the manager. He noticed that he had missed a few calls. "Pat? What does he want this time? Could he have any more information from his work as a private detective for him? Bill really didn't have a head for that after the meeting with the director. Everybody always wanted something from him. The great taxi driver, who always had new information. But this time he was the one who needed information about how to get to his daughter. Who could help him? The simplest solution, of course, would be Luc. But he would certainly not participate. In addition, the manager also explained to him that Luc should only be half trusted because of his past. The question that Bill kept asking him was what Luc could have done to keep his past so secret. But that didn't matter to him now. Berta was his only chance. But she was fired as the babysitter of her own children. It was a dicey situation. He had to think of something else urgently.

"Someone must hang this necklace around Beyonce's neck." He let his head sink into his hands. "Maybe I should call Pat back. After all, he's a private detective and knows tricks. He could certainly help me somehow," Bill convinced himself.

He called Pat back. Since he was on his lunch break, they agreed to meet spontaneously. Bill found a good place and sent the address to Pat.

By the time Pat was finally out of breath after twenty minutes, Bill had already ordered three espressos and jumped down. He had hoped that the caffeine would clear his mind, but instead felt the tension that had been with him all day turn into a restless nervousness. Perhaps he would have preferred to stick to tea. "Hey Bill! Please excuse my delay. Something important came up." Bill pulled the corners of his mouth into something he hoped resembled a smile. "No problem! How are you doing?"

"I'm fine and you?" Bill was silent for a moment. He needed help, but he didn't want to tell Pat that Beyonce was his daughter. He hoped to learn something useful through detours.

"I can't complain. Only Chris and Luc are on my neck. They want to meet me all the time and that might be annoying," he finally said.

Pat nodded understandingly. "I feel the same way. "

"Are the two also so attached to you?"

"Yes. Just a few days ago I had a meeting with them," Pat said.

"And what did they want to know from you?"

"Quite a lot."

"What does that mean?"

"They have mentioned many things in connection with the ongoing investigation. For example, the letters sent by unidentified persons to those affected after the abduction of the children."

"They asked me the same thing."

"Did they also ask you a question about the old lady and the 'Suitable liquid'?"

"Yes, they did. But what is that supposed to be? Suitable liquid?"

Pat thoughtfully knocked his index finger against his lip.

"I've never actually heard of a 'suitable liquid'," he said slowly. "From a 'magical liquid' on the other hand, yes." Bill was surprised. Because he had heard the expression 'magic liquid' before in connection with his tattoo. He remembered that a tattoo artist had taken the term into his mouth. He didn't understand it even then. His curiosity rose.

"Interesting. Do you know what that is?"

"I don't know."

"And then how do you know about it?"

"A friend of my mother's dropped the term once."

"And how did she know about the magical fluid?"

"She is a chemistry expert and has developed many mixtures. Many liquids with different properties".

"A chemistry expert?"

"Yes. Why, do you know her?"

Bill took a sip of his fourth espresso. When he had his features under control again, he said, "Could be."

"Can you describe them? Was she in a wheelchair, perhaps?"

"Yes exactly," Pat shouted.

"Did she have any other peculiarities? For example, a fire scar on her left hand?"

"Yes, that's right," Pat said astonished.

"I knew it," shouted Bill, "it's Mama Pee."

Pat shrugged his shoulders. "I know her by another name," he said and continued: "How do you know her at all?"

"Before I started working as a taxi driver, I was a bus driver for people with disabilities. I drove them several times then."

"Then you certainly know where she lives, don't you?"

"That was all a few years ago. I forgot her private address. But I still know the company she worked for very well."

"And the address of the company?"

"I don't know it by heart. But I could find my way there. Back then, you had to park your car about five hundred meters away and then walk on."

"Aha. I understand. It would be very nice if you could take us there. Luc and Chris will be very grateful to you for that."

"Why do you want to go there personally? With Luc and Chris, I can understand that."

"Because of my missing mother," Pat revealed in a hushed voice. His eyes shone. Bill made a stunned face.

"Again? You had asked me about it several times in the past. I thought you had finished after your stepfather said she was dead."

"No. I told you she disappeared when I was a kid. When I completed my training as a private detective, things always seemed strange to me. So, I decided to continue researching secretly. I found out that my stepfather's name was Duc. He is also the owner of the clinic where the children of Berta and Luc were exchanged. I also learned that many investigations are ongoing against him."

Bill swallowed. "Wait a minute. He's the owner of the Happy Baby Born clinic?"

Pat nodded. "Why?"

"Just so." Bill overplayed his concern. "Go ahead."

"Well, the background to my interest is that the chemistry expert was a very good friend of my mother's. I am sure that when I see her, she can tell me something helpful. Maybe she knows where I can find my mother. My stepfather claims that my mother is dead. But where is her corpse? I never got an answer to that."

"Now I understand you better."

"Would you then take us to her? Or at least Luc and Chris? They also help me with this investigation. Chris thinks that there might be a connection between my mom's disappearance and the exchange of children."

Bill thought for a moment. "What do I have to win? If his stepfather is the owner of the Happy Baby Born clinic, he certainly knows a lot. For example, who is behind the exchange of children. Maybe he also knows who manipulated us so that we can't remember our children! I think it will be worth it. I could use Pat more often later."

"No problem," Bill finally said. "Next week, when I'm on vacation, we can all go there together."

"That's really sweet of you."

Pat's cell phone rang. He took a look at the display.

"Answer it," said Bill.

"It's not a call. Just a memory. I have an important appointment soon. My lunch break is over anyway".

"No problem. I'm already glad that the appointment worked so spontaneously."

"Thank you," Pat replied and stretched out his hand to say goodbye.

17 When Luc stepped into the apartment that evening and took off his coat, he immediately noticed how Lea changed her facial expressions abruptly. "Oh, God! Hopefully she won't start that again," he thought. She sat on the living room couch and sulked. Luc pretended not to notice her sinister face, kissed her forehead and let himself sink to the coach next to her, where he opened the daily newspaper.

"Dear darling, your dress looks wonderful on you," he said lightly. Lea deflected the corner of her mouth.

"How was your day?", Luc continued.

"Very good," she replied bitingly.

"Wonderful," he replied and delved into his reading.

"I have news."

"Hopefully good."

"I found a new babysitter."

"Already?"

"Well. I just urgently need help with the children." "Well..."

"When does she start?"

"Tomorrow."

"What do you know about her?"

"Not more than you do. I had already forwarded her e-mail with her curriculum vitae to you." Luc distorted his face with anger. "I told you that I didn't want her. What is so difficult to understand about that?"

"Why not? We're not looking for a flirt partner for you."

"Leave it! I explained to you that she reminds me of a woman I met several times during an investigation. She was often under suspicion herself."

"Yes, but you also said that her name was different. Some people just look similar."

"You rather only do what you want," Luc rumbled. He stood up, pulled his e-cigarette out of his coat and left the living room.

18.. The next morning, Lea's face lit up. "Finally, I get support again!

After the dispute with Berta, I looked for a new babysitter for a long time and finally found one. Katy, this name sounds nice. Hopefully I like her work as well as her first name." The screaming twins ripped Lea from her mind. She quickly changed her diapers and fed the children. She looked at the clock. "Where is she? She's already ten minutes late." Her palm became damp. "She doesn't make the best impression for the first day. Actually, I have to get to work." It rang. "Well finally," Lea whispered nervously. She put the babies who had fallen asleep in their bed in the living room. Then she opened the door.

"Hello Katy."

"Hello Lea., Sorry for the delay. There was so much traffic."

Her eyelid twitched. "No problem. That can happen. Please come in."

"Thank you so much for choosing me," Katy said with a smile on her face.

"Nothing to thank," Lea said as she put on her coat. "After our last conversation, I was sure you were the right person for the job." Since the two children had just fallen asleep in the living room, they went into the kitchen.

"I was very happy when I read your e-mail and especially contented that I was allowed to start working today", Katy said.

"That makes me happy", Lea said distractedly. "I actually have to go. Please take good care of the children. They are my one and everything!

"Do not worry. I learned how to deal with children years ago. I love taking care of children," Katy replied with a smile.

Lea suddenly had a queasy feeling in her stomach. Katy's smile seemed a little too broad and she herself a little too cheerful. Then she called herself to order. There was no reason to distrust Katy. She had shown good references and seemed to be an all-around normal, nice person. It was the stress, quite simple. The stress could drive anyone crazy.

Lea took a look at the clock hanging on the wall. "Oh, I really have to go now! The white closet in the corner contains everything you need. In the top row you'll find hipp glasses. In the bottom drawers are clothes, diapers, and so on. In the middle are medicines."

"All right."

"I have another very important request for you, "Lea said while already on the doorstep. "Don't allow anyone to see the babies without my permission!"

"That's self-evident."

"Please be very careful. The environment here is not the safest!"

"So bad?"

"Children have already been kidnapped here several times," Lea asserted.

"That's terrible," Katy shouted, "I'll definitely keep it in mind."

"Besides, you should know that I live here with my husband Luc. We had a little argument and then made up our minds to keep our distance. But he comes by every now and then to see the children or to pick something up. Don't be afraid if he comes by."

"Okay. Thanks for the hint!"

"Do you have any more questions," asked Lea, while already in the car.

"You work from 8 to 16h, right?"

"Yes, that's what I told you in the e-mail. Usually from 8h to 16h. But since I am still on parental leave and I am currently representing my colleague, it is only three to four hours a day. Today I will probably work until 12 noon. Is that okay for you?"

"Of course! That is not a problem. I just ask if something should come up."

"Great. Well, I'll get it now. See you later. Oh yes, and if something should happen, you can always reach me on my mobile." Lea drove away with screeching tires.

Katy looked after her and smiled gloatingly. She locked the door and made a call.

"Hello", someone called at the other end of the line.

"Hello Libresti. It's me."

"And?"

"Everything's fine. She just left for work."

"Good. And her husband?"

"He wasn't even there."

"Are you alone now?"

"Yes. But she told me her husband could come anytime."

"Don't worry. I'll go to the police headquarters where he works."

Katy pressed her lips together for a moment and turned her gaze away to look out the window. "No. Are you stupid or what?"

"You know me!"

"Please don't do it."

"Don't worry. I will only park nearby and wait. When I see him, I'll get back to you."

"Okay, please be careful."

"You know me" he repeated and said goodbye.

"See you later," Katy muttered just before she hung up.

19 She wasn't a celebrity, but she was at least as well known. Her clothing style was old-fashioned and very conspicuous. Armed with her walking stick, she appeared wherever she was least expected. Most called her 'the old lady' because of her appearance. USFler had been puzzling about her for generations. Some believed that under her inconspicuous appearance was the power of a clairvoyant who was passed down from generation to generation. Others speculated that it was an entire family conspiring against Mark Dabrator. Anyway, no one knew who the old lady really was. Those who attacked her with her prophecies were mostly overwhelmed because she spoke in riddles. She had earned various nicknames over the years. One of them was the "weaponless huntress". Humans were her prey. Usually these people were victims of a scam of the MD-group, although they didn't know anything about it yet. How the old lady managed to learn so much in advance remained her secret. Today her hunting ground was a school - the school where Lea worked. She stood in front of the school entrance and was obviously waiting for someone. It didn't take too long for her desired prey to appear. It was Lea.

"So, we meet again, right?" the old lady opened the conversation.

" Certainly", Lea replied quite unfriendly. The lessons had already started. She hurried on without further comment.

"Inexperienced eyes are often the cause of our blindness," the old lady shouted after her.

Lea stopped. She did not hear this sentence for the first time. The last time she had heard it was shortly before she had received the letter with the pictures of Luc and Berta in a hotel. If there was anything the old lady knew about it, then ... Lea turned around and went back. "Was that a message," she asked.

"Probably ...", the old lady replied.

She had known. Much talk and no substance. The old lady was completely crazy. But since the old lady enjoyed a very good reputation in the USF, she didn't dare to ignore her and to walk on again. "Oh so," she said sarcastically. "And is the message addressed to all passers-by or just to me?"

"One does not exclude the other," the old lady replied. She lowered the walking stick into the dust of a flower bed and drew something that was probably supposed to be two babies.

"What does that mean?" Lea inquired with a distorted face. Her heart was beating up to her neck.

"A picture says more than a thousand words," whispered the old lady as she smudged the picture with her right foot.

Not again, thought Lea, who had advised the old lady at her last meeting to see a psychiatrist. Why did she waste her time with this old nut? Passing by, she said, "It's nice to have seen you again, but I have to move on."

"Our meeting is no coincidence, if that's what you thought," claimed the old lady.

Again, Lea stopped. What had Luc said? There were people who had ignored the old lady's words and paid a high price for it.

"Did you follow me? Or did you wait for me here?"

"You're still asking questions that won't get you anywhere."

The old lady hobbled towards Lea. She breathed heavily and supported herself on a wall. Then she opened her handbag, which was hardly bigger than a fist. She took out two cards and handed them to Lea. After a short hesitation she accepted the cards. What did she mean by that again? Both cards were about the size of a business card. On the back side there was a logo printed on it that looked familiar to Lea. In contrast, the front of the two cards was different. On one card was a small sun with a date underneath. On the second card there was exactly the same date in the same place, but the sun was missing. Instead there were a few red and black drops below the date and a black liquid.

"Relax, young woman. Only then will you be able to understand the message."

"Excuse me, but I actually have no head for it. I have to go, unfortunately. I should have started teaching ten minutes ago."

"Hm, hm! You will have to listen sooner or later! But I'm afraid it might be too late then."

"Then it will be like that," Lea replied bitingly and entered the school building.

"I would recommend that you go home before lunch as long as your Bunbis are in the wrong hands," the old lady shouted after her before the door slammed behind Lea and cut off her voice.

20 Lea walked through the quiet building. No one was to be seen. She wondered. She called a colleague and found out that there was no class that day. Her colleague claimed that she had only heard of it by e-mail the day before. She also explained that she could not talk on the phone for long because she was already sitting in the room where the meeting would take place. She offered Lea to forward the e-mail to her if she had not received it for any reason. "The e-mail contains all the details of today's workday. You can get the address and topics directly from it," she said.

"But I can't get to the first session on time! The meeting point is on the other side of town. It'll take me at least thirty minutes to get there!"

"No problem, I'll tell the director. Take your time and just come to the second half in an hour."

"Oh, thank you, that's sweet of you, "Lea expressed. She plugged in her cell phone and headed straight for the car. At the exit she noticed that the old lady was still not gone. She ignored her and walked past her.

Then she suddenly stopped. In front of her car was written in red letters: "The business of mourning lives on stubborn people". Lea froze. Had the old lady written that there? Well, that went too far! But Lea remembered how accurate her predictions were in the past and that for a majority of the USF population it was a sin to ignore the old lady.

She drove around on the heel and ran to where the old lady was leaning over. She was drawing again. Lea slowed down. She drew again two babies in the dust of the flower bed. But this time not once, but twice! Once on the left side in front of her and once on the right side in front of Lea. There was a strong wind blowing from behind. But the women stood so that she could slow down the influence of the wind from behind. Lea looked at the picture in front of her. For some reason it shivered down her spine. Then the strange lady asked Lea to stop while she ran a few steps away. As a result, one of the pictures disappeared through the gust of wind and the other was still visible on Lea. "What is this," Lea asked and looked up. But the old lady was already a few meters away from her: "That's it! Make the best of it! "

"The best of what?"

"The Message," the old lady replied just before she got into a black car and was driven away.

But as usual Lea didn't know what to do with this message.

Lea pressed the red button on her cell phone display. As many times as she had called Luc in the last fifteen minutes, he just didn't answer. She drove her hand over her forehead to wipe away the sweat and pondered. Then she started typing an SMS. "Hello, please answer the phone. It's really important. I met the old lady again and didn't understand anything. Maybe you have some time and want to talk to me about it? Please."

Then she kept an eye on the clock.

After exactly forty-one seconds it rang. "Hello," Lea responded.

"Hello," Luc said at the other end. "I don't really have time. I told my colleagues that I was going for a smoke. So, I can talk for a maximum of five minutes."

"It's all right," Lea said. "Just listen, it's important. I met the funny old lady again. I had the feeling that she wanted to tell me something important again. Unfortunately, I didn't understand." Lea laughed nervously.

"What did she say?"

"Not much. She gave me two cards with logos on one side and some pictures and a date on the other."

"And else?"

"She drew pictures on the floor. The first picture was a baby that she erased with her foot again."

Lea gnawed at her fingernails.

"And what did she say about that?"

"Not much, only a picture says more than a thousand words."

"Strange. And the others?"

"The other two pictures actually looked exactly like the first one. Two babies, one in front of me and another in front of her. When she ran away, the picture drawn before her disappeared."

"How?"

"Suddenly a strong gust of wind came from behind."

"Oh so. And since you had stopped, the picture in front of you was not blurred? "

"Yes, so it was! Can you do anything with it?"

"Not really," Luc replied hesitantly.

"In front of my car it was also written in red: 'The business of mourning lives on stubborn people', " Lea added.

"Maybe I could tell you more when I see the cards, she gave you."

"Okay. That's what we can do. Actually, I have an appointment with my colleagues. But I think it would still be enough time to stop by. Your place of work is only ten minutes away by car. Do you think that could be organized?"

"I'll go to the office and let you know."

"All right. I'll be right on my way."

Lea hung up and barely took enough time to drop the phone into her pocket before turning the key, releasing the handbrake and driving away with squeaking tires.

21 Luc waited outside the police headquarters for his wife. Only a few minutes later, her car drove up and came to a stop with screeching tyres. He opened the passenger door and got in.

"Here are the cards," Lea said, as soon as he had closed the door and hurriedly stretched them towards him. He looked at them.

"Can you do anything with it now," Lea asked breathlessly.

Luc nodded. "The logo on the back of the card is the same as that of the Happy Baby Born clinic."

"You're right! I didn't even notice that earlier".

"The date on the front doesn't mean anything to you either?"

"Yes, it is. That's the date of birth of our twins," Lea said excitedly. "That I didn't notice that right away!"

"What the pictures on the cards mean, we learned at school. The subject was called 'B-Ana'. We got different pictures and had to analyse them. Of course, the teacher also helped us. Maybe the old lady thought that you had attended the school in USF30-50."

"Maybe. Can you please tell me what they mean," Lea asked impatiently?

"Where should I start?"

"With the first card. What does the sun mean? Joy, right?"

"Yes. If you look closely, there's a little sign under the sun."

"Yes, I see that."

"That's the sign of memory."

"So, is it summarized as 'sunny memory'?"

" Approximately so. If you take everything into account - the logo on the back of the Happy Baby Born clinic where our children were born and the date of birth on the front, I assume it has something to do with you keeping the day in sunny memory. In contrast, the red drops on the second picture mean blood. The black liquid under the drops stands for tears of sorrow, the 'black tears'."

Luc watched Lea wrap a strand of hair around her finger.

"But what does it all mean? What is the message?"

"I'm sorry. That's all I can say. Everything else would be pure speculation."

"Thank you anyway," Lea said. She had turned pale.

"Well, I'm going back to work," Luc said.

"Okay. I'll drive on then."

Luc got out. Lea left right away. He looked after the car until it turned onto the main road and was taken out of his sight.

22 After talking to his wife, Luc found it difficult to concentrate on his work again. He had been sitting at his desk in the office for over an hour and hadn't made any progress on his task today. He was worried that the old lady had visited his wife and even more apprehensive that the date of birth of her children was on one of the cards. He became warm, very warm. It made no sense to continue working today. He turned off his computer and started to clean up his things. Then he called in sick and left the office. Full of worries he drove to their shared apartment. When he arrived, he parked his car in the parking lot in front of the house. Since he didn't want to frighten the new babysitter, he first rang the bell. But everything remained silent. "Lea had said that she had hired a new babysitter. Where is she? Don't panic Luc," he thought. It could be that she had gone for a walk with the children. He took his key out of his pocket and unlocked the door himself. He made himself a coffee and took a seat on the sofa. After two long hours, he called Lea, who should be finished with her meeting by now.

"Hello," Lea answered after the first ring of her phone.

"Are you done with your work," Luc asked.

"Almost. Why?"

"I'm at home now."

"And?"

"Actually, I just came by to say hello to David and Beyonce."

"I know that you didn't come for me. Is there a problem?"

"Yes."

"What's going on? I told her about you and showed her your picture because I thought she might not allow you to see the children in my absence."

"That's not the problem."

"What then?"

"I've been waiting here for more than two hours and she's still not there."

At the end of the line there was dead silence.

"Lea? Are you still there?"

"She just started today. How can she possibly go for a walk if she's not familiar with our area?"

"I ask myself the same question. Even if she becomes familiar with the surroundings, it can't take that long! Didn't you tell her that the area is dangerous here?"

"Yes, I did," Lea replied tonelessly.

"Can you call her?"

"Yes, of course. I then hang up briefly and get back to you in a few minutes when I have called her."

"All right, thanks."

His worries continued to rise. He ran back and forth like a tiger in a cage and kept looking through the window, hoping to see a woman with a baby carriage. After another five minutes of restless up and down he decided to take a walk. He didn't know exactly what the new babysitter really looked like, but he knew his children and their prams. The street was empty. Only a few homeless people sat on a bench some distance away. After he walked down the street, his instinct came in.

From the apartment there was only one pedestrian route. The other route led to the highway. So, he would have to meet the babysitter if she was on foot with the children. He continued walking. The path left the settlement and led out into the open field. It was no longer asphalted. In the damp soil of the rain that fell last night, you could easily see all the footprints. After a long observation Luc had to admit to himself that the footprints on the ground were not those of a human, but those of a monkey. There were also marks of ducks and other birds, but no trace of a pram. A cold shiver ran down his back. When did Lea finally call back? In a moment it would explode! He made his way back. When he stuck the key into the lock, the phone rang inside. "Yes," Luc replied breathlessly after running through the hall at record speed.

"Hello, Luc."

"Lea?" he asked, surprised.

"Yes. Did you expect another call?"

"Why don't you call me on my cell phone?"

"I tried, but it was always your voicemail."

Luc took his cell phone out of his pocket and looked at the display. Only now did he realize it was off. He cursed. "The battery must be empty. It doesn't matter, now. Could you reach the babysitter?"

"It rings, but she just doesn't answer the phone."

Luc felt his worst fears confirmed.

"I hope for your sake that nothing happened to the children," he said coldly. He was about to hang up when Lea shouted at the other end: "Wait! She just texted me!"

Luc felt a stone fall from his heart.

"And, what does she write?" he asked.

"That she went for a walk with the children." Lea sounded as relieved as he felt.

"Where?"

"Near our apartment."

"That's not true at all," Luc shouted.

"What? Why not? "

"I was just outside myself. I know our area very well. I can assure you one hundred percent that she is not here!

"Well, if you think so."

"What does that mean? I explain the background of my opinion and all you say is 'well'?"

"You, I have no desire on stress. I'll do some things and then I'll get back to you when I get home."

"Quite great."

"Bye."

Luc didn't answer his wife anymore. He just hung up and threw the phone on the sofa. Then he left the apartment.

23 When Lea came home from work the same evening, she found neither Katy nor her children in the apartment. Panicked, she called her husband.

"Hey, it's me!"

"That's obvious! What is it", Luc asked coldly.

"The children are still not there ..."

Luc cooked inside. His feelings had been confirmed again. He tended to blame his wife for the whole disaster. If she had not quit Berta, it would never have come to this.

"Please say something ", she begged him.

"What should I say? I must painfully state that I must also pay the bill of your stubbornness again."

Lea was silent.

"From the beginning I was against you quitting Berta. You only let yourself be controlled by your emotions. As I keep telling you: A person who lets himself be steered by emotions is like someone driving a car drunk. Now we have the proof again. You trusted a woman out of rage. And now she has disappeared without a trace."

"Don't be so pessimistic! Maybe something just happened to her and the police will get back to you soon," Lea mentioned hopefully. But her voice trembled.

"I hope so. The most important thing is that the children should be well".

"Can you please come over?"

"Are you serious now?"

"Yes. Please. Let's put our marriage problems aside. The kids are more important than our ego." Luc put his hands on his hips and put his head at a slight angle. "Only if you keep your emotions under control, ok?"

"I'll do my best!"

"Good. I would need about an hour."

24 It would be an exorbitant understatement to claim that Lea was worried. She only now realized that something could really have happened to the children. She just came home from work, but she didn't even think about changing her clothes or taking off her shoes. She remembered talking to the old lady, also known as the "Goddess of Prophecy". Again and again she played the conversation in her head. No matter how often she played the sentences, the old lady's message was still unclear to her. But the bad feeling in her stomach area intensified. She ran into the kitchen, took a cooling pad out of the freezer and put it around her neck. When Luc finally entered the living room after an eternity she immediately jumped up.

"Has the new babysitter still not called," he asked. Lea was silent. She didn't know the answer to his question anymore. She pressed her thumb as hard as she could and finally said: "Not yet. But she'll be in touch soon."

"I hope so for you, because otherwise you have a real problem!

"What does that mean now?"

"You quit Berta against my will. And that even though the maternity tests proved that she is the natural mother of the children. You sent her away and if something happens to the children, it doesn't look good for you at all."

"Thank you! I already know that myself". Suddenly she could no longer feel the cooling pad that she had put around her neck. She was afraid that she would be accused of having taken the children away to hurt Berta or Luc. She remembered the threat of Berta to file a lawsuit at MixSKids. "If the kids are really gone, it looks really bad for me. Dear God, you are my witness. I had no bad intentions. Please don't let me down," she pleaded. Then she tried to reach Katy by phone for about a thousand times. Unsuccessfully. "Shit! She's still not answering," she shouted and peppered the phone onto the carpet.

"He who never listens seldom escapes the ring of suffering! Would you have listened to the old lady?"

"Spare your stupid sayings. I had enough of that when I talked to the annoying old lady."

"That's part of your problem. Everything you don't understand is stupid. As I told you before, try to follow her tips before it's too late."

"You're talking about the old lady as if you could just type her statement into Google and have it translated." How can you follow tips you don't even understand? She's always talking weird stuff."

"What did she say again?"

"I don't know, there were a lot of things I didn't understand. She said something with 'wrong hands'. I wouldn't have taken her tips from the last time seriously. And if you don't want to hear, you have to feel. And it could be too late. So stupid stuff!"

"I can't really explain what she means by that either. But from the lessons of the past, I know that she appears wherever danger is imminent. I recommend that you try to understand her statements. These are often important tips to follow in order to avoid the worst."

"I just don't understand why everyone here follows their word as if it were law! She is only a human being. She can be wrong sometimes. We don't have to worry now just because she told me that I should come home earlier."

"Are you serious? Did she really tell you to come home earlier? "Luc wondered.

"Yes, she had mentioned something like that", Lea confirmed disinterestedly.

Luc pulled his hair up.

"You don't understand," he said.

"No, I really don't understand. Unlike most USFler, I don't see her as a goddess of prophecy who deserves a good reputation. But as an evil old woman who manipulates people. As if she could really see into the future".

"That's your opinion. In the USF it's an honor to get a visit from this old lady. She has a very good reputation. And slowly I think that she wanted to warn you about this babysitter with today's conversation. Maybe she suspected that the children could be kidnapped. If you had followed her tips, it might not have happened at all."

"Had, would be, if ... You can always say that. It hasn't even been said yet that the children were kidnapped by Kathy."

Luc was silent. He massaged his temples. "I very much hope so," he finally said.

25 Two days later Luc was on the road with his colleague. Chris gave Luc a side glance. They were on their way by car to the meeting with Bill, but silence had reigned since they left twenty minutes ago. Chris had twice tried to start a conversation but was unsuccessful. Luc seemed to be mentally absent. It was strange that his colleague appeared in the office this morning with uncombed hair and cream on his face. Luc's shirt was also only ironed from the front and quite crumpled at the sides. As if Luc, who was otherwise very tidy and disciplined, had just taken a shirt out of the closet shortly before work in a hurry and ironed the front quickly. In addition, he smelled of alcohol.

Chris was a little worried about his colleague. "Everything all right, Luc?"

"Yes, of course. Everything's fine. Why?

"Really?"

"Yeah, if I tell you."

"Sure? Somehow you are different than usual."

"It can happen, can it?"

"Yes of course. But the way you appeared today, I seldom experienced you."

"What do you mean?"

"I mean the rest of the cream on your face..."

"Oh." Luc folded down the little mirror and stroked the cream from his face. He laughed forcedly." I was in such a hurry this morning that I didn't even look in the mirror."

"Ah yes. Now I also understand why you didn't notice that your shirt was wrongly buttoned."

Luc took a quick look down at himself.

"Shit," he grumbled. "Thank you."

"Very much gladly. You can always talk to me openly."

"Your destination is in a hundred meters on the left side," said the navigation device.

Chris wondered. He looked at Luc questioningly. "Is this the right address?"

"Yes. I typed in the street Bill sent us by SMS."

"Do you know why he wants us to meet at the cemetery?"

"I don't know."

They stopped and got out. While Luc thoughtfully stopped next to the car, Chris went searching a few meters further and typed Bill's number into his mobile phone.

"Hello?"

"Hello Bill. We're already there. We're standing in front of the cemetery with the car."

"How? Which cemetery?"

"Cemetery MK."

"I don't know that one. I'm sitting in the café waiting for you."

"Wait a minute. Dabratorstrasse twenty is right, isn't it?"

"No. I don't know them. I sent the address to Luc by SMS."

"Okay. All right. I'll get back to you later."

"Wrong address", Chris said dryly.

Chris checked the address. He was boiling inside. "How could you mistype yourself like that? The entered address does not even resemble the one in the SMS."

"Sorry, colleague. Everything is going wrong for me at the moment." Without further comment Chris entered the correct address into the navigation system. "Now it should be correct. There was a moment of silence again. Chris secretly looked at Luc from the corner of his eye. "What can burden him so much that he entered a wrong address? And is it a coincidence that the address is this cemetery? I remember that an important person in his life was buried in this MK cemetery. But now is not a good time to address it," Chris thought.

On the way Luc's mobile phone rang. He pulled it out of his pocket, took a quick look at the display and then threw it next to him. "Women are just indispensable devils," he said. The phone was still ringing. Chris took a look at the display. "Lea! That's your wife."

"Right."

"And why aren't you answering? Maybe it's important."

"I don't think so."

"If you say so." Luc was silent.

"Lea hasn't been able to reach the new babysitter since her first day at work," he said. "And the worst part is that David and Beyonce are out with her."

"Oh no! Since when exactly have the children been missing?"

"For more than forty hours."

"Already? Should we call colleagues and start a big search?"

Luc gave his colleague a sharp look. "That's not possible. Otherwise I would have done it long ago. "

Chris frowned. "Why not?"

"After the change of the old law a period of at least forty-eight hours is presupposed in the USF."

Chris nodded. "That's right. I had forgotten that. And what are you going to do now?"

"I don't know. In eight hours, we can inform our colleagues," Luc said dejectedly.

"What exactly happened," Chris asked. "If we think together, maybe we can find a clue where the babysitter might have disappeared to."

Luc told his colleague everything.

"I can't get rid of the feeling that she was trapped," Luc concluded.

"Your wife?"

"Yes! Think about it: the new babysitter disappears on the first day with the children. This must have been planned long ago! It's not that easy."

Luc looked out of the window. "Do you think the disappearance of the children might have something to do with Mark Dabrator?"

Chris looked at him in horror. "It's possible. Especially if you assume that Geo was kidnapped at Berta's because the kidnappers thought the child was her biological child."

"That's exactly my concern. Maybe the kidnappers somehow found out that my children are Berta's biological children. So, they sent someone to pretend to be a babysitter to kidnap the children."

"People who don't know what Mark Dabrator is capable of, may think your guess is unrealistic. But I think it's possible. There have been cases where the group has had their spies trained in different areas and professions".

Luc had turned pale.

"Excuse me. I forget that you're personally affected this time." Luc waved off.

"Everything you said, I thought already."

"What do you want to do now?"

"If only I knew. Do you have a suggestion? "

"I would first of all still wait. If you don't hear from the babysitter and the children by tomorrow, the city should be alerted."

"And if it's too late?"

"I don't think so!"

"Where did you get this assurance? You said that the baby would be sacrificed four weeks after receiving the letter?"

"Yes, at least that's what I thought," Chris said meekly. Luc was silent and stopped without a word next to the café where they had an appointment with Bill.

26 Bill was just a taxi driver to a lot of people. When his fellow students asked him why he had decided to take a taxi after an excellent study, he always replied: "Out of sudden love". Only a few members of a secret group to which he belonged knew the true background. While waiting for Luc and Chris in the café, he looked down at his father's little Polaroid photo, which he carried everywhere in his wallet. A single human life was of little value, he had experienced for himself. Dad, he thought, you always warned us about Mark Dabrator and his allies. Mama asked you several times to move away and to keep your hands-off politics. But you never read to get away from your goals. You followed without fear the fight for a democratic USF. It cost you and your family lives. Only I survived. When I came home that evening and saw your bodies on the ground, I realized for the first time how cruel your opponents were. I wonder if I should admire you for your determination and courage. Or whether I should hate you for never listening to Mama and for destroying our family with your fight against Mark Dabrator and his allies. Thanks to the old lady I escaped. I've left the city, changed my identity and now I'm secretly continuing your fight. Hopefully I will make it. Please father, give me your energy and your courage. I will need both. Bill wiped his cheeks that had got wet for some reason. Then he carefully put the tiny photo back into his wallet and rose. As he stepped outside, the two policemen just got out of the car.

"Hello Chris. Hello Luc. It's nice that you're finally here."

"Sorry for the delay. I really appreciate you waiting so long for us despite everything," Luc replied.

Bill nodded.

"You wanted to tell us something about the ongoing investigation. On the phone you said it might be of the utmost importance."

Typical Luc! He didn't talk around the bush for long. "Yes. At my last meeting with Pat, he told me that you were looking for a chemist. Maybe I can help you."

"What do you know about the chemist," Luc asked.

"Not much. But I've often driven a woman she might know."

"Driven? Was she your customer?"

Bill hesitated. "Yes, you could say so. But that was some years ago. I hope she still works there."

Luc rubbed his chin "How many years are we talking about?"

"The last time I drove her was three years ago."

"And where does she live," Chris asked.

"I don't remember that anymore. But I still know for sure where she worked at that time! "

Chris folded his forehead. "The woman had a disability, right?

"Right."

"Is she the chemist we're looking for?"

"No. I guess she can help find the chemist."

"How far is it from here to the place where she works," Luc asked.

"I guess it takes about ninety minutes by car."

"And the address? "Chris had pulled out his notebook.

"I don't know it by heart. But I know how to get there."

"Would you show us the way then?"

"Of course. I'd have time now if it's good for you."

Luc seemed surprised. He exchanged a look with Chris. "I have to make a quick phone call. A moment please."

27 While Luc rushed back to the car, Chris steeled himself inside. Now was the time to talk to Bill in private. "There's something I've wanted to ask you for a long time," he said.

"What's it all about?"

Chris already knew from Berta that Bill could be very sensitive to some issues. And the topic he wanted to discuss with him was one of them.

"It's about Mark Dabrator."

"Sorry. I'm afraid I can't be of any help," Bill said frostily.

"You don't even know what I want to ask."

"It doesn't matter. I have no interest in answering your questions on this subject."

Giving up was out of the question for Chris. But he also knew that pushiness would not lead him to the desired conversation. He would try again later. There was a freezing silence until Luc came back.

"Thank you for waiting, Bill. I have another appointment in about an hour. So today it is unfortunately impossible for us to go to the address with you, as the trip there and back alone would take three hours. And depending on how long we are there, it could take even longer. It would make sense for us to keep half a day free for this. I would like to suggest a few appointments by SMS after work. Then you can let me know if one of them suits you as well. Is that all right for you?"

" Yes, that's ok. "

"We have to move on now. Thank you very much again and goodbye."

Bill called Luc after him: "I'll wait for your message...".

28 About an hour later, having returned to the police headquarters, Luc left it immediately after an emergency call. Chris took a look at the diary that Luc had quickly pressed into his hand and found that Elvira was to be interrogated by Luc that afternoon. He and his brother's girlfriend didn't have the best relationship yet! But it didn't help, he had to represent Luc in his absence. Chris looked at the clock. The interrogation was scheduled for three o'clock. It was five to three. He still wondered how Sebastian put up with such a woman. But it was his life after all. He was a policeman and had to stay professional.

When Elvira entered the room, Chris had put on his professional face. "Hello. Glad you could make it."

She squeezed a nod. He was aware that it annoyed Elvira that he always kept a certain distance from her despite family ties. For him, she was a woman, as he had told his brother, who had a bank account instead of a heart. He did not get rid of the impression that love played no role at all in Sebastian's and Elvira's relationship, but only of financial interest.

"I have an appointment with Chief Inspector Luc," she said.

"Unfortunately, the Chief Commissioner had to leave urgently after an important call."

"That's typical again," she snarled. "Why didn't he call me to cancel or postpone the appointment? "

"The Commissioner asked me to wait for you and represent him at the interview. Please follow me." Chris walked into the interrogation room ahead of Elvira. This room was equipped with a lie detector and four different cameras. "Please have a seat."

He waited in silence until Elvira hesitantly sat down and then also sat down on the chair opposite her.

"As you already know, this is about little Lea. Your partner has indicated that you have something to do with the kidnapping of his daughter Lea. What do you think? Before you answer, I must inform you that our conversation is being recorded. It could also be used later as evidence in court. This room is also under video surveillance."

"What do you want from me?"

"The truth!"

"The last time I told you everything I know."

"Then I would ask you to repeat everything you said. So, we have your statement once and for all."

"I did not kidnap Lea!"

"Nobody said that."

"What then?"

"We just want to know if you know more about the kidnapping of Lea."

"No! How am I supposed to know more?"

Chris pushed his office chair closer to the table and supported himself with both elbows on the table. He watched Elvira closely. "I'd love to get the answer from you!"

"Listen, Commissioner, when Lea was kidnapped, she was not alone. My son was also kidnapped in the end."

Chris rose. "Exactly, that seems strange to us. Then why was he freed and Lea not?"

"How should I know that? As far as I know, that's part of your job."

Chris let himself sink back into the chair and leafed through a few documents that were already on the table.

The documents also included pictures that Sebastian had taken of his daughter disappearing with Elvira's business partner. Next to it stood a box full of bills that had been sent by post to Elviras and Sebastian's address after the kidnapping.

Sebastian had taken the money to the police headquarters immediately after he had received it, and the responsible laboratories had examined it for finger pressure.

"Let's talk about the money that was sent to you after the kidnapping."

"What about the money? Sebastian and I have handed it over to you in its entirety!

"Exactly, that's it! Then how do you explain that your fingerprints were on some of the bills?"

"What ... I beg your pardon?"

Chris saw the fine hairs standing up on her forearms.

"You have already understood me correctly. Our laboratory experts checked and confirmed it three times."

"I can't explain that to myself. Maybe I touched some notes by chance."

Chris didn't let up. "One might believe that. But how is that supposed to work if you brought the banknotes here untouched? The money was wrapped in two transparent foils and was still completely closed. Or did you open and close it again?"

Elvira stood up. "What do you mean by that?" she asked coldly.

"Sit down before I help you," Chris said. "Here I ask the questions!"

"How do you talk to me?"

"In your own interest, answer only the question. Save yourself any counter-questions. Otherwise, you can spend the rest of the day in a cell."

"You are not allowed to do that! There is no evidence against me."

"Yes. But according to the USF law, you are not allowed to disturb the work of the police in any way. If you resist interrogation, I can keep you here from forty-eight hours to three months."

Elvira hesitated. Chris moved the files just bored out of hand. "What is it now," he asked. "I have the next appointment soon. So please hurry up!"

Elvira sat down in her chair. All of a sudden, she seemed very small. "Please, believe me, I am innocent."

" Well, please help me to prove your innocence."

"How then?"

"By answering my questions, and honestly!"

"But if I don't know something, then I can't say anything about it, can I?"

"What can you tell me about the businessman, Sebastian ..."

He was promptly interrupted by Elvira: "He has nothing to do with it."

"Let me finish, please."

"You don't need that at all. I already know what you want to say. I can assure you that he has nothing to do with this."

"Pay more attention to what you say! You say he has nothing to do with the kidnapping. Then how do you explain that Sebastian was able to show us a video in which this man was traveling with his daughter?"

"Such bullshit! Who sees his missing daughter on the way and makes a video of it instead of running after her screaming? You don't believe that yourself."

"Whether I believe in it or not, I can probably decide for myself!"

"Excuse me. I'm just trying to make it clear that Sebastian is just imagining the whole thing."

"An imagination that can be seen on a video?"

"He's an outstanding computer scientist."

"And?"

"He can make a fake video like that."

"Don't worry. We also have experts here who check our videos for authenticity. And I wonder why he should do that at all? Would he have any other reason to blame your business partner?"

"Could be. Sebastian once met me in a restaurant when I was talking to my business partner. Sebastian immediately thought that something was going on between the two of us. But this is not the case. It's all business."

Chris wasn't surprised that his brother didn't really trust her. He had observed Elvira for a long time and was able to get a good picture of her in the meantime. She was a woman who was always looking for a better offer. However, this was his personal opinion that had nothing to do with the case. "What do your business relationships look like?"

"He owns a car dealership. If we need cars for the company I work for, such as at company parties or when a business partner comes from abroad, we rent them from him for a good price."

"And wouldn't you have to conduct these business talks in the company?"

" Sure, in principle. But since we understand each other so well, we meet now and then in a restaurant to talk about our business and also about private topics."

 "And you wouldn't have to do this in the company?"

Chris raised his eyebrows. "You just said that your meetings are always purely business?"

"Yes, and? Don't you ever talk to your colleagues about your private life?"

"What topics are you talking about?"

"That's none of your business!"

"In this case it is! It is a private matter. Do you talk about your partner's daughter?"

"No, of course not."

Chris did not answer. Instead, he gave her a sharp look and pulled up his laptop.

"Is the conversation over now?" Elvira asked annoyed, but there was a slight tremor in her voice. "I have to go."

"Just a moment. Then you can go."

"I've already told you everything."

"Please take a quick look," he said and turned the laptop so she could see the video.

Elvira slapped her hands in front of her face. "What is that?"

"You can see well, can't you?"

Silence.

"He had a video camera at home and never told me about it? That's going too far, I'll report him. He is depriving me of my privacy!"

"The video clearly shows two important things. On the one hand, that you are lying. And on the other hand, that you also have something against Lea. Am I right?"

Elvira rose. "At this point, I want to end the conversation."

"That's not for you to decide."

"I won't say anything until I've talked to my lawyer."

"Very well. But under these circumstances, I can' t let you go. There is evidence that you have something to do with the kidnapping. We will keep you here until that is cleared up. Then the courts will decide how to proceed with you."

He pressed a button.

Elvira had turned pale.

"I am innocent," she said, "Chris, please believe me!

She reached for his hand. Chris took a step back and freed himself.

"It's not up to me to decide," he said. Two policemen appeared.

"Take her away," Chris ordered.

29 Chris typed his fingers on his desk while waiting for Sebastian to answer. A click sounded as someone picked up the phone, then Sebastian's voice came on from the other end: "Yes?"

"Hello, Sebastian. Something happened that you should know."

"Did you find Lea? Where is she? Can I pick her up?"

"No, not yet. I just had a conversation with Elvira."

"And?"

"She didn't want to tell much without first consulting her lawyer."

"Is she gone yet?"

"No. I had her locked up in a cell."

"Oh brother, did that have to be? I just wanted her to say what she knew about the kidnapping and help us bring Lea back home."

"With the video, there is enough evidence to suggest that Elvira is involved in the kidnapping."

"Yes, I know. But we are a family. You could certainly have made an exception."

"Sebastian. She is our main suspect in this case. I couldn't just let her go."

"You never thought much of my relationship with her. But you are also a human being and know what it is like. Emotion and reason rarely fit the same pot. "

"But what would you do if you were me? I am a policeman. Besides, your daughter's life is at stake."

"You're right. Then how does it go on?"

"I don't know yet. If she decides to answer the questions, then I can let her go. But if it turns out later that she testified wrongly, she will be punished harder."

"And if she does not testify?"

"Then she'll stay in the cell."

"How long?" asked Sebastian in an anxious tone.

"Unfortunately, I can't say that."

"Alright, brother. I love Elvira, but my daughter is of more worth to me."

"There is something else. When I showed Elvira the video, she doubted the authenticity. She said that you would run after your daughter and certainly not make a video if you saw her with someone else."

"That's also true. Did you not tell her how the video was made?"

"No. She doesn't need to know my source. Besides, the video was taken by one of those drone cameras. Since the drone was still being used during a trial, I'm not sure if it could be accepted in the USF as evidence in court."

"You see! I already told you when I handed you the suitcase that the drone and my software could help in many investigations."

"Enough of the publicity."

"Okay. Contact me anytime you need my help."

"Something else..."

"Yes?"

"Elvira wants to charge you with the other video for robbing her of her privacy. I have to admit that this could be punishable. We have to come up with something good."

"Don't worry about it. The video was taken in my private office. Elvira wasn't allowed in there at all."

"If it was in your private workroom, then it's really okay because she's not employed by you."

"All my employees know about the security camera. It's part of my home, but it's only for work. Some meetings take place there. Actually, Elvira makes herself liable to prosecution if she takes the keys to my workroom in my absence and hides there to make phone calls."

"That's right. Another proof that she has something to hide. She certainly didn't want to talk on the phone in the living room or somewhere where the kids could listen."

"Exactly my guess."

" Well, I must attend other appointments immediately."

"Okay. Thanks for the call and see you later."

"Very gladly. See you later."

30 Elvira was restless. It was the first time she had sat in a cell. Cold sweat ran down her back. She had been taken away from her cell phone and given a replacement cell phone, which was monitored by the police. She had been told that she could reach her lawyer or family member. Nothing more. Her talk time was no more than five minutes per hour. All the numbers were stored by the replacement mobile phone and could only be deleted by experts with the help of a certain software. All this had been communicated to her when the policeman had locked her in the cell. "Shit," she thought. Who could she call anyway? She had played the brave one in front of Chris. A lawyer, my ass. She didn't have a lawyer. She couldn't afford one anyway. Her heart beat faster. Could she call her boss? No, then the investigators will immediately suspect that she might have something to do with it. Sebastian wouldn't answer the phone anyway. For him, only his daughter mattered. Maybe it is better just to tell the truth, otherwise, she would have to stay in the cell much longer. In the end, she would have to testify anyway. Then she thought about how Chris had looked at her during the conversation! Oh, dear God, he wouldn't make her life easy. It was an opportunity for him to let his hatred of her run free. Unlike Sebastian, she couldn't fool him. What was she going to do now? Full of excitement she asked the guard to call Chris. It took exactly twenty-five minutes for him to appear in front of her cell.

"Did you decide otherwise?" he asked.

"Yes. I will testify," Elvira replied angrily.

"Follow me, please."

"Back in the room where everything is recorded?"

"Yes."

"Does that have to be?"

"Do you have a problem with that?"

Elvira pressed the jaws together and remained silent.

"Please sit down," Chris said when they arrived in the interrogation room.

Elvira sat down on the chair on which she had also sat during the first conversation. Her hands trembled slightly. She folded them together and put them between her legs. "After this, I can go home?"

"If you answer everything, yes. Before that, you have to sign a statement that you will not leave town until everything is cleared up."

"Will I get my cell phone back?"

"Enough with the questions. You remember where we ended the first conversation, right?"

Elvira was silent for a moment.

"Sebastian recorded this video without ever telling me," she said soundlessly. She never would have believed him to do anything like that. She felt her tears coming. "Sebastian only had eyes for his daughter Lea. He gave her everything. She always came first. I had to agree with everything, whether I wanted to or not. Even if he wanted to go out with me or if he wanted to give me something, he had to ask the little nag. Only when she gave him his consent could he take an evening off. I tried everything to win her heart. But no. The last time she told me that I am not her mother and that I can never be a substitute mother for her. Who can bear such an arrogant and loveless girl?"

"And that's why you thought about how best to get rid of her?"

Elvira shook her head energetically. "No, for God's sake!"

"I'm sorry, but everything speaks against you!"

Elvira slid restlessly back and forth on her chair. "I admit that I know more than I've told you so far. But I won't testify until Sebastian is there."

"That is not a problem. I'll contact him and make an appointment for next week."

"That would be good. Thank you."

"Before that, I would have one more question."

"Yes?"

"Who is this someone who has managed to win Lea's heart in such a short time?"

"I beg your pardon. In the beginning, you talked about a kidnapping and now about a love relationship?"

"Yes. One does not exclude the other! But I wasn't thinking about a love relationship, although it's possible. What I want to express is the following: How did it come about that she shines like that after a kidnapping?"

"How should I know? Why don't you ask Sebastian? He finally made the video!"

"What do you know about your business partner?"

"As I said, I want to tell the rest only in the presence of Sebastian."

"All right! Give me a few minutes."

Chris took his cell phone and called Sebastian.

"Hello Chris," Sebastian reported.

"Hey, brother. Hopefully, I'm not disturbing you at work?"

"No. I couldn't make it for the last few days. My head is only filled with thoughts of my daughter. I left my office this morning. I'm home now and trying to rest."

"I understand. Well, Elvira is sitting in front of me again. She doesn't want to answer another question until you're here. Would you be able to come in the next half hour?"

"Of course," Sebastian replied very quickly.

Chris was surprised. He hadn't expected Sebastian to have time so spontaneously. It was also the first time that his brother got involved in such a spontaneous appointment. He made his lips smile thinly. "Wonderful! I'll send you a link right away. When you arrive, press it. This will give you information about the room and how to get there."

" Alright. I am on my way right now."

After the phone call, Chris put the phone on the table. He looked at Elvira. She played with her hair and chewed her fingernails. He briefly immersed himself in thoughts. How could it be that Lea looked so happy on the video? Mark Dabrator just can't be behind it! Surely it had to have something to do with these rich men who spoil children and fake their great love. The twelve-year-old Lea was in puberty. Was the man her lover? A pedophile? Hopefully not! That would have been a psychological disaster for my niece! Or had Lea left voluntarily? Did she feel neglected by her own father? Did she feel like Elvira that he had too little time for her?

About twenty minutes later, there was a knock at the door. Chris opened.

"Sebastian! It's nice that you could come so quickly."

"No problem," Sebastian replied. He gave Elvira a brief look and contemptuously distorted the corners of his mouth. She stroked her hair behind her ear and smiled embarrassedly. Then she looked down.

"Can we finally proceed with the interrogation," asked Chris.

She hesitated. Her lips trembled. "Yes," she finally said quietly. "His name is Gai," she continued. "He is the manager of a car dealership. As I said before, he has nothing to do with me directly, but with my boss."

"Spare us these boring details. Where is Lea? And why do I have to be here?" Sebastian shouted. She avoided his gaze quite casually. "I know where she is."

Chris swallowed. Sebastian was stunned. He stared at her with a rapid heartbeat and an open mouth. "You're not serious, are you?" he shouted in horror.

"Everything with calm, brother. Why don't you tell us where we can find her?"

"She is with the most famous and richest woman in the USF," she replied briefly.

"Queen Natasha," Chris inquired.

"Yes," Elvira confirmed.

Sebastian jumped up. "That can't be true." His eyes shimmered moistly.

"I was so wrong about you. How could you do this to me? Since the beginning of our relationship, I told you the whole story. You know that Queen Natasha was against my relationship with her daughter. You know that her daughter moved away with me against her will. She had no more contact with her mother until she died. Lea is the only thing I have left of this beautiful soul. Yet you dare to take her away from me?"

Elvira was silent.

"How can you see me suffer? You experience it very closely how the whole thing destroys me. I can neither eat nor work. All this time you have been trying to persuade me that she is dead?"

"Sorry. I don't want to embellish my stupidity. But I only did it because I was ordered to. Queen Natasha is a powerful woman and friends with my boss."

"Wait a minute. Did you know that Queen Natasha is Lea's grandmother," Chris inquired.

"Yes, Sebastian had already told me. It was stupid of me. But I really had no bad intentions. I knew she was fine. I just took the opportunity to get more attention from Sebastian."

"How ridiculous! And that's why you told me that she had already been destroyed by Mark Dabrator," Sebastian replied, "Why don't you tell us how much she paid you to destroy my soul? "

Elvira was silent again. "I'm sorry."

Sebastian turned to her with flaming eyes. "You should be locked up. That's where you belong. It's over between us! I should rather have listened to my brother earlier." Then he left the room without further comment and slammed the door behind him.

Chris asked Elvira more questions and had her locked in a cell at the end.

31 After the interrogation with Elvira and an unexpected visit of the old lady, Chris called his colleague directly.

"Hello, Luc." But in the background, it only roared, "Can you understand me?"

"Hello, Chris. The connection is not so stable, but I can hear you."

"I just finished interrogating Elvira."

"And?"

"Finally, she admitted it."

"Well done, colleague."

"Thank you."

"Is there anything else?"

Luc sounded strange. He had already had the same feeling in his stomach when Luc left the police headquarters.

"What's going on with you? You didn't even tell me who made that distress call or what it was all about."

"The distress call came from my wife."

"What is wrong with her?"

"She received a letter with an address. A very important address that could take away all our worries."

Chris became curious. "An important address? So maybe the old lady is right again?"

"What do you mean?"

"She came straight to me after Elvira had left."

"What did she say?"

"Nothing. But she left you a gift. "

"Great joke! It's not my birthday."

"I mean it seriously. If you want, I can open it now."

"Yes, please! "

"Maybe the old lady took a new job at the Post Office," Chris joked. He took the parcel, cut the tape and opened it. There was a coin in it. Chris turned it back and forth so that its shiny surface reflected the light of the lamp.

"It's a coin, but not a normal one," he said. "It has mirrors on both sides that are absolutely identical. It has a diameter of about ten centimeters." The connection broke off. Chris dialed Luc's cell phone number, but unsuccessfully. After a few attempts, he gave up. He put his cell phone on the table and waited for Luc to call back.

32 Luc was still alone in the car. Only five minutes had passed since his conversation with Chris had been interrupted due to network problems. Despite numerous attempts, he couldn't reach Chris again. He put the mobile phone on the side seat. He was still thinking about the conversation with Chris. Especially the gift Chris had mentioned. Luc, in contrast to his wife, was firmly convinced that the old lady never appeared anywhere by chance. He didn't think she was crazy either. In the course of his long career, she had repeatedly appeared in cases and had left hints to those affected. And she was never wrong. The problem was to decipher the clues in her own language. "It is typical of her to convey coded information," he thought. What, for example, did she mean by the coin? When his cell phone rang again, he picked it up in a flash.

"Is it you, Chris? Where were we?"

"At the coin."

"Okay. And what's engraved on it?"

"Nothing!"

"Then what did you mean by the old lady being right?" Luc asked in surprise.

"She was wearing a jacket with the 'curly mark' at the back."

"What on earth is the 'curly mark'?"

"It's time for a tutorial again," Chris joked.

"Yes, please. You're the specialist in this field."

"According to my grandfather, the 'curly mark' is a unique language that is not written with letters, but with special characters."

"Did your grandfather teach you how to understand the language?"

"Yes. Not perfect, but I could understand what was written on her jacket."

"And? What does it mean?"

"The next person to receive my gift will also receive a letter that has a seemingly important meaning."

Luc was affected. He wondered if the anonymous letter that his wife had received had been sent by the old lady. Luc bit his lower lip. "Apparent?" he asked. "What does that mean in concrete terms?"

"By "apparent," it often means everything that does not correspond to the truth. Unfortunately, I cannot say it more precisely. But I would advise you to ignore the letter," Chris said.

"How am I supposed to do that? After all, the letter is about my kidnapped children!

"What exactly does the letter say?"

"I haven't read it myself yet. But my wife told me that the letter had an address where I could find our children."

"And you believe in that?"

"Believe? What is believing?" Luc asked desperately. "Do you know what I have believed in to this day?"

"No. Maybe you'll tell me."

"To a God who provides justice and not to one who only makes me suffer."

"Okay," Chris said quietly.

"But the time to believe is over. What I believe doesn't matter anymore. You know what's happened lately. My wife accuses me of cheating, and my children have been kidnapped. For me, my family is my everything. She is the reason that I enjoyed going to work in the morning and earning money. A living dream that became a nightmare within seconds. And now you speak of faith?"

"Luc, please calm down ..."

"I don't want to calm down! It is my children who have been kidnapped, and therefore, no matter what awaits me there, I will go there."

"Then let's make a plan together and go to the address together."

"Unfortunately, it is far away from here. I still have no idea how and what... But I have to go there, and I have to go there immediately."

"I have a bad feeling."

"Do you have a special reason?"

"I'm afraid Clan Mark Dabrators might take advantage of your condition to get you out of the way."

Luc slowed down. He was torn back and forth. He parked the car in a parking lot near a gas station.

"My decision is made," he said. "I'll go there."

"Luc, listen to me. We've been working together for a couple of years now. I know how important your family is to you and I know how long it took for Lea to get pregnant in the first place. I have great respect for your willingness to take every risk to save your children. But seriously, do you think the only way to paradise is through hell?"

"Do you know another way?"

"It's only a matter of time before we find another way."

"You don't understand that. I am at the end. The nights are torture. Instead of sleeping, I roll around in bed and worry about my kidnapped children. Worrying about my family. I just have to do it. Even at the cost of my own life."

"Okay. If you need help, get in touch with me."

"Thank you!"

"But please also give me the address so I can prepare some units for the emergency. You never know ..."

"There's no correct address! There are only a few coordinates where I can find a green car. I'm gonna have to get into this one. I'll find out everything else there."

"Maybe the meeting point is already stored in the navigation system. If this is the case, please let me know."

"I don't think whoever sent the letter will make it that easy."

Chris was silent at the other end. "Be careful," he said then.

33 Luc stopped his car in front of his house with a full brake and squeaking wheels. For a moment he remained motionless and let the telephone conversation with Chris go through his head again. Then he got out.

When Luc stepped into the living room, Lea looked up surprised.

She stood paralyzed opposite him, the letter in her hands. Her gaze was firm, but her nostrils trembled.

"Is this the anonymous letter you were talking about on the phone," Luc asked.

"Yes."

"May I have it for a moment?"

Lea stretched out the letter to him.

While Luc was reading, the corners of his mouth were pulling downwards. "I have to make a quick phone call," he said on the way to the study.

"Hello Luc," Chris answered at the other end of the line.

"I have the letter."

"And?"

"The letter was written using a computer, not by hand."

"Too bad. But clear that Mark Dabrator does not give himself such nakedness. What does it say?"

"I can't get the address in advance. Tomorrow three different people will call me to tell me the city, the street, and the house number in that order. The letter also mentions that "the duration of a call must not exceed fifteen seconds."

"I am not a psychic. But I still think it's a trap."

Luc was silent.

"Luc, please. Don't let your emotions lead you through this alone."

"From my point of view, there's nothing to argue against except the old lady's visit."

"I see more."

"What else?" asked Luc and drove through his hair with one hand.

"All the descriptions correspond to ingredients that are often only used in the kitchen of the Mark Dabrator Clan. A five-star cuisine whose food must not be served to connoisseurs or hungry people."

"Please speak in a language I can understand."

"Danger! They've designed everything so you can't plan anything against them in advance."

"Exactly! And for this reason, it is logical not to take any risks. Who knows, maybe some of them have even been on duty for the police before."

"What do you think about taking a hidden micro-camera with you?"

"The letter says that they installed special sensors and detectors in the car. I'm not allowed to use a phone or anything similar as long as I'm in or near the car. A hidden camera makes no sense here. We would be discovered immediately."

"Those are important details you've been hiding from me so far."

"I'm sorry. It's a long letter."

"That's why I'm proposing," Chris continued grimly, "to follow you in secret."

"How are you going to do that without getting caught?"

"There is always a way."

"I'm sorry Chris, but I don't want to take any risks. It's about my children. I would never forgive myself if anything happened to them."

Chris was silent.

"Thanks anyway. I'll keep all the information you gave me in mind," Luc continued, just before he was about to hang up.

"I wish you much success and strength," Chris replied and hung up.

34 Luc returned to the living room after his phone call with Chris. He had something on his mind that he wanted to get rid of. He called to Lea a few times and searched the whole apartment unsuccessfully. Then he called her on phone. But she didn't answer the phone either. He sat down at the dining table and wrote her a letter. Then he put the letter next to the flowerpot on the table. Before he left the house, he went to the shelf to get a picture from the family album. But the album wasn't where it used to be. He searched unsuccessfully in a few other places. Finally he gave up, packed the car keys and left the apartment. He opened the car, but as if to delay the inevitable, he took a last look towards the garden. There, behind the hedge, stood a pram. It was her second, which Luc had bought as a replacement for the emergency. He rubbed his eyes, but the pram was still there. Luc closed the car again and slowly approached the pram. He clenched his sweaty hands to fists. It was actually hers. The marking on the side was attached. He looked around nervously. "Lea," he shouted out loud.

"The voice sounds like your father's," a soft voice sounded. He ran further into the garden. "Lea, is that you?" he shouted again.

"Do you hear, children? That sounds like Papa, right? "

Luc ran around the corner and discovered his wife under a tree. She sat there with two cuddly toys in her arms that belonged to her twins. She held one in her left arm and the other in her right. She pressed both to herself. Luc slowed down. Lea sang the twins' favorite song. Whenever she played it on her cell phone, a smile had spread on the faces of David and Beyonce. Luc stopped and closed his eyes. He thought of the time after the birth when he had played with his wife and their two children in the garden, and they had exchanged happy looks exactly in the same place. He opened his eyes again and slowly approached Lea. She was still singing. Luc got goosebumps, as he squatted across from her. Tears ran down Lea's cheek.

"Everything will be all right," he said and felt tears shooting into his eyes too. She was still staring down at the twins' cuddly toys. "What's the matter with you, my darlings?" she asked. "Is Mama singing so badly today? Why don't you laugh like usual?

"Mama sings very beautifully," Luc said. "Maybe they're already asleep." Finally, he managed to catch her gaze. She looked at him with a fixed gaze. "I sang it all the time. Neither of them even laughed once," she repeated. Luc wiped his wet cheeks and pulled his smartphone out of his pocket. He was looking for a recording he had taken a few months after birth when the children had laughed out loud for the first time. "Do you want us to try it together again," he asked. "Maybe they like it when Mom and Dad sing together."

Lea nodded. While they were singing together, Luc left his finger on the play button. He waited for the exact spot that the twins loved most and then pressed play. The twins' laughter resounded. Lea opened her eyes wide. A slight blush rose into her cheeks, and a smile spread across her slightly open mouth. Luc wiped away her tears. When the recording was over, Luc said, "The children are tired now. Let's go home." He lowered his eyes to the two cuddly toys and pressed his lips together. Then he shook her hand and helped her get up. As they stood in the living room, Luc looked at his watch. He said, "Please take good care of yourself. I have to go now. I wrote you a letter. It's on the dining table. Everything in it is true."

"Okay," Lea said while keeping eye contact with him.

"See you soon," Luc hardly said. Then he turned around and ran to the front door. As he put his hand on the door handle, Lea shouted, "Luc!

Luc waited.

"Thank you."

Luc pushed the handle down and stepped outside.

35 Lea was alone again. She supported her head leaning against the door. Oh, if I could turn back time,' she thought. Everything was perfect. And now what?

She went into the kitchen and made herself a hot chocolate. Then she returned to the living room and opened the letter Luc had written to her and sat down on the sofa. She wondered how heavy the envelope was. Next to a folded sheet of paper, there was a chain and a USB stick in the envelope. She unfolded the paper and read the first sentence. "You know me," it said. "Where I come from, people believe more in promises than in God. Can you remember our conversation the night after our wedding? Then you told me how much you loved me and that you would never survive if I betrayed our love. My answer was short: 'Where I come from, promises are never broken.' You didn't believe me then. But I was very serious. Where I come from, we had to record every promise in writing or on an audio file. Those who did not keep their promises had to expect many years of imprisonment or even death, depending on the promises they made. Today it is different, but not in my heart. That has shaped me very much. What I want to make clear to you is that I never promise anything for nothing. Promises have something to do with honor and not with one's own ego. Surely you can count on one hand how many times I have promised you something in the last ten years, can you? They were exactly four times. The first time was when I promised to marry you. The second time we got married: 'I will stick with you, for better or for worse.' The third promise I made to you was: 'I will remain faithful to you as long as you remain faithful to me.' And the last promise I gave you after the birth of our children. I will always be there for my children. I will always protect them, even at the cost of my life'. You wonder why I remind you of it? Quite simply: Today is the day. It is the day I will prove to you how serious I am about my promises. I'm leaving, and when I get back, I'll have the kids with me. Chris said, and also the old lady, that it could be a trap. But my decision has been made. I can no longer watch how much you suffer. And I can no longer sleep with the constant worry that our children will be abused or even killed by foreign hands. I would rather die trying to save my children than be accompanied by a bad conscience all my life. Since I don't know when or if I will come back, I wanted to get rid of a few things. Better now than never! I want to tell you that I never had a sexual relationship with Berta. I swear to you on my life. If our problems have anything to do with Mark Dabrator, I can't confirm yet. In the envelope, you will also find an old chain and a USB stick. I got the chain from my mother before her death. In the medallion, there is a key that opens a secret suitcase. The suitcase can be opened with three keys. The keys have a number on the front. In our case it is number two, so one and three are missing. So, if you see someone with a similar chain, speak to them. If I don't come back, I ask you to put on the chain and wait again at the entrance of the school, where you met the old lady. I firmly believe that she could do something with it. Even if you don't think much of the old lady, please do me a favor. On the USB stick, you will find several folders. In the first folder called 'Our Sun,' I have uploaded videos of us: all the beautiful time we spent together. In another one called 'EinigSchaffenwiralles,' I'm talking about that one evening that you were desperate after the doctor's visit and I convinced you that it would eventually work with a child. There's also a folder called 'Thunderstorm' where I tell you about the pain, I've felt every day since we've been separated. Then there's another folder called 'Foreverwithyou.' It contains video recordings of me, which are meant for David and Beyonce. Please play them later when they are big, if I don't come back. I still love you very much, and that will never change. Some parts of this letter may be sad. But that's not necessarily a bad thing. I am still the same. You accused me of sometimes being cold with you or of trying to teach you. I apologize for that. Nobody is perfect. The most important thing is to consider the sensitivities of others, especially when we know them. All the best, my darling. Hopefully, see you soon." The letter slipped out of Lea's hands. There was so much she wanted to say to Luc at that moment. But Luc was gone, and there was nothing she could do to get him back.

36 Lea just bent down to pick up a packet of baking powder that had fallen out of her hand when she saw Katy in the baby section at the end of the hallway. She gave a choked scream, and the baking soda fell out of her hand again. Instinctively she tried to hide behind a shelf. Was she dreaming? She wiped her face and shook her head in disbelief. She had come here to do her weekly grocery shopping, more to distract herself than out of necessity, and then her former babysitter, the kidnapper of her children, just stood there as if nothing had happened. The blood was rushing through her veins. She gasped for air and looked at the woman again at the end of the corridor. There was no doubt. It really was Katy. She slammed her shopping bag on the floor and wiped her sweaty hands on the jeans. Then she shot down the hallway in a fury.

"See you again," Lea said coldly. Katy slowly turned around to her.

"Lea," she asked with a frozen smile.

"I hope for your sake that my children are as well as your eyes seem to be."

Katy turned around contemptuously and continued rummaging through the table.

" Are you not ashamed of yourself?" Lea shouted. Her voice became louder and louder. Instead of answering, she just sparkled at her in silence. They exchanged bitter looks for a moment. Lea was about to explode. She clenched her hands to fists and opened them again. She would have preferred to jump on her and beat her up until she told her where she had taken the twins. Instead, she pulled her cell phone out of her pocket and typed in the police number. As soon as she put the phone to her ear, her interlocutor took a menacing step towards her.

"Who is that?" Katy asked.

"Hello," Lea said into her mobile phone without paying any attention. "Yes, please."

She gave the address of the supermarket.

"What does it look like?" she asked and collapsed the phone.

"The police?"

Lea kept a close eye on Katy. If she tried to escape, she would stop her.

But Katy didn't make any effort to run away. "How naive are you?" she asked, "Your husband is also a policeman. Surely one of the most experienced in the USF. He and his colleague Chris together have more successes in investigative work than ever before in USF history. Right?"

"Yes. And?"

"I wonder how you got the idea to contact your husband's colleagues where he failed himself."

"I forbid you to talk about my husband in that tone!"

" Well, the truth hurts? "

"Shame on you! Shame on you, you devil!" Lea shouted. "Have you no heart? How could you have kidnapped the twins? "

"Sorry, but I must go now."

"No way!" Lea approached her. "You're not going anywhere. If you think you can escape with your pretended composure, you are wrong! Do nothing stupid, otherwise, I will alert the whole business. Believe me, without my children I won't let you go!"

The supermarket door opened and two policemen entered.

"The police are here!"

"Very well done, Madam Commissioner. I'd better stay here with my hands tied and wait for the handcuffs." Lea did not pay attention to her. Instead, she waved to the policemen.

"Now it's over," she said.

"I just wonder why you always believe so much that they can help you. Even though you know that they can't prevent what's supposed to happen."

Lea truncated and then gave her a questioning look.

"Hello," one of the policemen greeted the two women. "Which one of you called us?"

"I called," Lea shouted.

"How can we help?"

"This is the woman I recently hired as a babysitter. She disappeared on the first working day with my twins!"

"Can we please see your IDs?"

"Here you go." Lea was the first to give them her ID.

"Yours too, please."

"Here." Katy also gave her identity card to the second policeman.

"You are Lea, and the other woman is Katy. Right?"

"Exactly," Lea confirmed.

"And she was your babysitter?"

"Just one day. Then she disappeared with my children, as if she had planned it from the beginning. In spite of several requests she did not tell me where I could find my children!"

"We would like to take you to the police headquarters and clarify all further details directly there."

"Of course! She should be locked up," Lea shouted.

" Is she coming too?" Katy asked and looked over at Lea.

"Yes, we'll take you both with us," said the policeman.

Lea hesitated, then she gave herself a jolt. She had nothing to lose after all. "What are we waiting for?" she asked.

" Ladies first."

37 During the journey, there was peace in the car. Lea took her cell phone and wrote Luc an SMS. "Hello, Luc. Thank you very much for the letter and the nice words. I would be happy if we could sit down soon and talk about everything in peace. The real reason I'm writing to you now is that I accidentally saw Katy shopping and alerted the police. We are on our way to the police headquarters. Please let me know when you have read my SMS." She pushed her cell phone back into her pocket. There was still silence. Lea took a look at Katy. Why does she seem so relaxed? It almost seemed as if she was suppressing a grin. But she certainly only imagined it. Those were the side effects of the stress of the last days. Her phone rang. "Hello Luc," she reported. And suddenly it got restless in the car.

She watched as the driving policeman sucked in the air and Katy's mimic changed abruptly. "Do you hear me?" Lea asked.

"Which presidium are you going to," Luc asked sharply.

"I don't know. Wait, I'll ask," Lea said and turned to the policeman in the passenger seat.

"Which presidium are we going to?"

The policemen looked at each other with wide open eyes and gave no answer.

"Can you please tell me to which presidium we are going?" Lea repeated a little louder.

"What is going on," Luc's voice sounded from the listener.

"They say nothing."

"Give one of them the phone, please."

"Okay." Lea stretched out her cell phone to the side driver. He took it and lifted it to his ear. "Yes, hello."

"Hello. This is Chief Inspector Luc, responsible for all areas in the USF 1-30. May I know who I'm talking to?"

Silence. "What should I say now," the policeman whispered to his colleague at the wheel. The driver made a gesture, and the passenger hung up.

"What are you doing?" Lea shouted.

"What is it?" The co-driver rumbled.

"Why do you hang up? And why don't you give me my cell phone back?"

"Quiet," the driver shouted and gave Lea a menacing look.

Lea sank back into her seat. She froze. Suspiciously, her stomach was flat. She was silent until the destination.

Herstellung und Verlag:
BoD – Books on Demand, Norderstedt
ISBN: 978-3-7494-5145-6